HOOD ROYAL

VALENCIA WARREN

VIKKI M HANKINS™ PUBLISHING

VMH

Vikki M. Hankins™ Publishing
3355 Lenox Rd. NE Suite 750
Atlanta, GA 30326
www.vmhpublishing.com

Manufactured in the United States of America

ISBN: 978-0-9984553-7-2

10 9 8 7 6 5 4 3 2 1

Cover Design by VMH Vikki M. Hankins Publishing
Cover Photography by Dewayne Jones
Cover Models: Alicia Warren, Shondrella Dixon, Erica Dixon
Cover Model Stylist: Valencia Warren
Author Photography by Vikki M. Hankins

HOOD ROYAL

ROYAL IS, YOUNG, HOT AND PRESTIGIOUS. SHE'S
GUARANTEED TO KEEP YOU WANTING MORE

Chapter 1

I woke up at six o'clock in the morning to get ready for school. It was kind of cool outside but nothing was going to stop me from wearing my true jeans with my black halter top. I was basically a spoil brat, I didn't have a father but my mother worked her fingers to the bone to get me whatever I wanted, some people may call it privileged but I like to call it hood royal. What is hood royal you ask, well let me just explain hood royal is when you live in between the hood and the boondocks, I mean you not rich but you not poor. I mean don't get me wrong my mom and I stayed in a house but she never told me no. My name is Royal Wilkinson but my friends call me Ro-Ro. I'm seventeen years old and soon I'll be graduating from high school. I don't know if I want to go to college or anything but if I do I want to go wherever my home girls go because we made a promise to never break our circle in pre-k and trust we were going to stick to our promise. I made it on time to get on the bus but I had to wait two more stops before my girls got on. I went all the way to the back of the bus because that was where the royal girls sat. I laid back and relaxed. Five minutes later I was being greeted by my friends.

"Hey girl what's popping?" Terri asked

Terri was the loudest one out of everyone but she was also one of the meanest ones out of all of us. Terri was light skin, about 5'7, she was slim but she had curves and those long legs that every man drooled over Terri had her mother and father in her life. Her father was a lawyer and her mom a doctor so if you thought that I was spoil I was nothing compared to her

"Nothing girl but this party that I keep hearing about," I said.

"Ohhh a party finally some fun," Kiera said.

Kiera was the funniest out of everyone but don't get it twisted because she could get serious when it was time. Kiera was dark brown, about 5'3, with an hour glass figure. Kiera also had both of her parents in her life but her mother was the bread winner and so her dad had no say so in her upbringing and whatever her mother said went, so you could imagine what Kiera's life was like.

"Girl you already know that we on the top of the list because ain't no party without hood royal," Star said.

Star lived with her aunt and uncle because her mom was on drugs and nobody knew who her father was. Star was Golden brown, about 5'5, with an hour glass figure but she had the breast to go along with it. Her aunt was a director and her uncle was a producer and they both did anything for Star because they didn't want her to feel different from any other kids that had parents so of course you already know that she was the most spoiled out of everyone.

Then there was me my mother was a surgeon and I was the only child so of course I got whatever I wanted. I was 5'7, thick, with hips that had the men drooling and crawling on their knees. Everyone felt that I had the biggest heart out of everyone and I would give the shirt off my back and to be honest I would because one day I would hope that someone would do the same for me but I also had a bad side and as long you stayed on the good you wouldn't have to worry about the other side.

"You already know," we chanted together.

"So where is the party going to be," Star asked.

"Decatur," I replied

"Girl you know I loves me a house party," Terri said.

"Girl please you love any kind of party as long as it's a party," Kiera said laughing.

"I know right," I said.

We talked some more on our way to school but not before we were rudely interrupted by Jeff and his crew. Jeff was what we like to call a rich stuck up want to be hood. He stayed in a mansion on the other side of town but he wanted to go to Atlanta high to try and fit in.

"What's up sexy ladies?" Jeff asked.

"Not you again," Terri replied.

"There's only one me baby, so check this out we was really coming over to see was ya'll going to that party tonight."

"We don't know yet but why is that any of your business," Kiera asked.

"It's our business because we would like to escort you fine ladies to the party."

"Not even if you guys were the last men on earth" Star said as we all started laughing.

"And who said you were invited anyway I'm sure mommy dearest wouldn't like to hear that her sweet little boy is in the hood," Terri said.

"What moms don't know won't hurt," Jeff said.

"Boy please mama got a tracking device on that ass," I said laughing.

"Royal don't even down play me like that you know I got my ways of making it to a party." he said.

"You down played yourself now shoo fly" I replied

Finally, we made it to school and thank goodness because Jeff and his crew were really starting to get on my nerves.

"Look I'ma catch up with ya'll later," I said.

"Okay," Kiera and Star said

Terri and I had a class together so we begin walking. We made it to my class and I couldn't even focus I mean today was the last day of school. I wanted to jump up for joy.

"Pss."

"Girl what's up."

"I'm ready to go it's so boring in here," Terri said.

"I know but what did we expect its history."

"I understand that but I wasn't born in the eighteen hundreds so why should I care what happened then?"

"You should care because sooner or later one of us is going to do something big and we going to be in the history book and those students will feel the same way about us."

"No, they won't because I'ma make mines interesting."

"(Laughing) you special and not in a good way."

"Yea I know so, what are you wearing to the party?"

"I don't know yet but whatever it is it's got to be fly."

"You know it do because you never know who will be there."

"Nobody that I care to see I'm sure of it."

"Probably not yet."

Chapter 2

The whole day it felt like time was moving so slow but when that bell rung to let us know that it was time for lunch. That was the time that my girls and I got together and talked. When we made it into the cafeteria we grabbed a tray and went to our table and yes, I said ours. Everyone sat at different tables every day but everyone knew that we owned the back table.

"So, what's up for tonight, do everyone have a date?" Kiera asked.

"Well I for one feel that it's better if we all go alone because you never know who you will leave with," Star said.

"I don't have a date either but it's not because I plan on leaving with anyone," I replied.

"Oh, girl you so stuck up," Terri said.

"It's not that I'm stuck up I'm just hard to please, but anyway what time are we leaving."

"Well my mom getting off at six and by that time I should be ready so I say that we leave at eight," Terri said.

"Okay so do everybody have something to wear?" I asked.

"You know I do I got something for everything," Star said.

"Me too," Kiera agreed.

"Well I got to hit up the mall so I'll just go right after school," Terri said.

We talked a little more before we left to go back to class. I must admit out of the whole day there was nothing better than the bell ringing to let everyone know that school was over with. I was the first one out of the class and the first one on the bus. My home girls and I talked the whole bus ride and when we made it to their stop we parted. When I finally got off the bus I ran home only to find out that it was empty. I went inside my closet to find something to wear and I came across my pretty, royal, blue, strapless, Dereon dress with my royal blue wedges and I called my best friend Star.

"Hello."

"Girl what you doing?"

"Girl I'm trying to find me something to wear."

"Well I already found me something."

"So what are you wearing?"

"I can't tell you because then I will have to kill you, na'll for real though you'll see."

"Heifer."

"I love you too."

"Whatever, so who are you hoping to see?"

"I'm not hoping to see anybody special."

"What about Juelz?"

"Girl ya'll the only one going crazy over that boy."

"But he so irresistible!"

"To ya'll but not to me."

"Okay we going to see but look I got to get ready because Terri's mom let her drive the car and she said that she leaving the house at eight."

"Okay well I'll see you in a little bit."

"Okay."

I got off the phone took a shower and got dress I had just gotten a new weave and I just had to curl it so I curled my hair and did my makeup. At eight-thirty-five Terri pulled up with Star and Kiera in the car.

"Hey ya'll," I greeted when I entered the car.

"What's up?" they said.

"Girl you looking fly," Kiera said.

"Thank you but we all looking fly," I said.

"And you already know," we all said.

After a half hour drive we made it to the party and it was popping I mean everyone was there. We went walking and making our way through the crowd and we finally made it to the table where the food and the drinks were but I was interested in neither. I stood there trying to act like a lady but when my favorite song by Lil Chuckee came on I almost forgot that I had on a dress. My girls and I got on the dance floor and all eyes were on us. And then Star started to smile.

"Omg there go Juelz!" Star said.

"So," I said.

"Girl you know he fine," Terri said.

"And you already know," they said.

"But I'm not going to act like I'm melting."

"Umm but just look at him," Kiera said.

Juelz was about 6'2, light skin, a fade, perfect teeth, and a nice body, and a sexy face to match but I needed something more to keep my attention

"Don't you just want to bite him?" Star asked.

"No, I'll pass," I said.

"Girl whatever I know that I'll take me a piece," Terri said.

"Enjoy, but enough about him I'm hot I'm about to go and get me something to drink."

"Okay we'll be waiting right here," Terri said.

"Okay."

I went to the table to grab me something to drink when I was approached by this tall brown skin brother he wasn't normally my type but he was a nice-looking guy

"Hey Miss Lady would you like for me to get that for you?"

"No thank you I got it."

"You don't have to be afraid I don't bite."

"I'm not afraid that's not in my nature."

"My name is Flight."

"I'm Royal."

"It's very nice to meet you Royal."

"It's nice to meet you too."

"So, Royal when are you going to let me take you out?"

"We just met like 5.2 seconds ago."

"Exactly and the only way to get to know me is a date."

"True."

"So, can I get your number?"

I wrote my number on his hand.

"I'm going to call you."

"Okay."

I walked back over to where my girls were standing.

"So, who was that fine brother?" Terri asked.
"His name was Flight and he asked me out on a date."

"I thought you said that you weren't looking for anyone special," Star said.

"I wasn't he approached me."

"Well I'm ready to go because the eye candy is gone," Star said.

"Let me guess Juelz."

"Yes," she said.

"Girl you pitiful."

"If you had the chance you know that you would take it."

"Honey please he will have to bring more than just a pretty smile."

We stayed a little while longer and then we left. It was only nine-thirty and neither one of us was ready to go home so we got into the club with our fake id. When we made it inside the club was jumping. We begin dancing and making our way to the dance floor.

"Attention groupies there's ya'll man Juelz," I said.

"Yes, it is," Terri said.

"Ya'll must be stalking him, how did ya'll know he was going to be up here?" I asked.

"Okay I got to admit I did over hear him say he was going to be here," Star said

"Star really?"

"Well I don't blame you girl," Kiera said.

"I know that's right," Terri said.

"Ya'll I got to go to the girls' room but I'll be back."

"That's fine we just going to watch our man."

I walked to the restroom and it was empty I was so happy because I always hated a crowded restroom. I came out of the stall, washed my hands, and exited the bathroom and to my surprise someone was outside waiting.

"Hey pretty lady."

"Hey Juelz."

"How do you know my name?"

"Everyone knows your name especially the women."

"Is that a good thing or a bad thing?"

"I don't know whatever floats your boat."

"So, were the things you heard about me good or bad?"

"It's good for someone like you."

"What do you mean someone like me?"

"I mean the ladies man."

"I'm not a ladies' man."

"Is that why I hear your name all over town?"

"I can't help what people say, look the reason why I was coming over here is because I saw you at the party and I liked what I saw."

"Okay."

"You sassy, what's your name."

"Thank you, and its Royal."

"(Laughing) Na'll for real Ms. Royal I didn't want to disrespect your man so I watched from a distance."

"Who Flight?"

"Yea Flight."

"Well he's not exactly my man yet but he did ask me out."

"So, I still got a chance?"

"Juelz it's going to take more than a pretty face and a smile to catch my attention."

"Oh, but you ain't said nothing but a word."

"We'll see."

I walked off and I left him standing there. When I finally made it back my home girls were waiting for me.

"We saw you over there talking to Juelz so what was you guys talking about?" Terri asked.

"Nothing he was just telling me that he likes what he sees."

"So, you guys are going out now?" Star asked.

"No I told him that I'm not like the rest of these girls those looks are not going to work on me."

"Well if it doesn't work on you it definitely will work on me," Star said.

"You need help."

"No, you the one need help how can you turn down someone as fine as Juelz?" Star asked.

"Because it's got to be more to a relationship than looks and until I find that kind of person those other men can stay where they are."

"Girl you just missed out on something special," Terri said.

"Well if he so special he'll come back."

"Well Juelz is not the type to keep chasing women, look how good he looks he can have any women that he likes," Terri said.

"Well if he wants me he will and if he doesn't then the other women can have him, now let's go party because I'm tired of talking about him, I came to have fun not talk."

We got on the dance floor and we begin dancing again. We dance the whole night and we left at eleven o'clock. When we left, I saw Juelz and his crew sitting on the hood of a car.

"Hey Ms. Royal," I heard Juelz say.

"Yea."

"Don't forget what I said."

"I won't if you won't."

"That's a bet."

We got in the car and left, Terri dropped me off at home, and I tried to sneak into the house but when I opened the door.

"And just where have you been?" My mother asked.

"I was at the movies with my friends," I said.

"What did you go and see?" she asked.

"A haunted house 2," I replied.

"Well the next time call me and let me know."

"Okay ma."

"Are you off to bed?"

"Yea after I take a shower."

"Okay."

I went in to my bedroom sweating I couldn't help but to think what would have taken place had I not thought of a lie that fast I had to be more careful. I took a shower and I laid down to get some sleep but then I received a text from Flight.

"Are you sleep?"

"No at least not yet."

"Can I take you out tomorrow night?"

"Where are, we going?"

"It's a surprise."

"What time?"

"Eight."

"Okay I'll be ready."

"Okay goodnight sleepy head."

"Goodnight."

I closed my eyes and went to bed. The next morning, I woke up to my mother calling my name.

"Yea."

"What are you doing today?"

"Hanging with the girls"

"Well make sure you call me if you're going to be late coming home."

"Okay ma."

I went to take a shower, got dress, and made breakfast."

After I was done I called Terri.

"Hello."

"So, what's up for today?"

"I don't know have you talk to the other girls?"

"No not today."

"Okay well I'm about to call them and then I will call you back."

"Ok."

Chapter 3

I hung up with Terri and I waited, an hour later she called me back letting me know that there was going to be a party tonight. I was fine with that but I let her know that I wouldn't be able to stay long because I had a date. After speaking with her I called Flight to let him know that we would be going on a date from the party he didn't have a problem with it so all I had left to do was to find me something to wear. After getting everything together I sat and watched television most of the day. At six o'clock I was leaving to go to the party.

"Ro-Ro why can't you change your date for tomorrow?" Star asked.

"Because that would be rude."

"Come on its not like he's Juelz," Terri said.

"He's not and that's why I like him because I won't have to worry about all these groupies around."

"Well I would love to have a man that everyone wants," Kiera said.

"Why so when he gets mad at you he can go to one of them for what he feels you're not giving him instead of trying to work it out?"

"Whatever girl you don't know what you're missing," Terri said.

"Nothing apparently and why are ya'll all up in my love life anyway where are ya'll men?"

"Our men are at the party waiting for us," Star replied.

"Good so worry about ya'll and stay out of mine."

"Well, excuse us," Kiera said.

"Ya'll excused."

We finally made it to the party and it was so crowded I mean everyone was there, the music was jumping, and everyone was having fun. I got on the dance floor and I began to dance. I was having so much fun that I forgot that anyone was around but when a slow song came on it brought me back down to earth. I left the dance floor and when I turned around I could see Juelz hanging with his crew and he was watching me. I walked towards my friends while in the middle of our conversation.

"I thought you might need a drink after dancing on the dance floor."

"Thank you."

"No problem Ms. Royal."

"So, what is this?"

"What is what?"

"You bringing me a drink?"

"Oh, you said that actions speak louder than words so this is part of my action."

"Oh, ok and what do you want in return?"

"Oh, I don't want anything in return because I guarantee you that what I want is what I will get."

"And what's that?"

"In due time, you will know."

And he walked off and left me standing there. I mean what he said was pretty good but no man was going to have my mind all twisted up in knots. I went back to partying still thinking about what he said. I could still see him watching me from across the room. At eight o'clock Flight showed up to take me out. I said good bye to my girls and we were off." After an hour and half ride later we finally pulled up to a building."

"Where are we?"

"This is my homeboy house he invited my date and I for dinner."

"Why didn't you tell me?"

"Because it was a surprise"

"But I don't know what to talk about."

"Just be yourself."

He got out the car, came around, and opened my door. I didn't want to get out but I managed to tell myself that it would all be over soon. We made it to the front door and just when Flight was about to ring the doorbell a car pulled up.

"Oh, that's him now," Flight said.

I sat and waited for the person to get out of the car, when he finally did he was an okay guy in the looks department. I watched as he went to the other side of the car and opened the door for his date. After helping his date out, the car he finally made it to the door.

"I thought you stood me up bro" Flight said

"Stood you up nigga you ain't on no date with me so I couldn't have stood you up."

"(Laughing) Nigga you know what I mean."

"Yea I guess."

"Oh, my bad lil mama I ain't mean to be rude, ah Stone this is Royal my date, Royal this is Stone my right-hand man."

"Nice to meet you Stone."

"Like wise."

He introduced his date to us and then we entered the house when we made it inside it was nice but you could tell that it was missing a woman's touch. We went straight to the dining area and sat at the table talking and getting to know one another until the food was served. After the food was ready we said grace, continued talking, and eating. After dinner, we watched a movie and when it was over we left.

"So, what did you think about Stone?"

"He's really nice and funny."

"Yea me and him knew each other since elementary, our brothers grew up together and they were best friends and we did the same."

"That's how it is with me and my girls."

"Yea that's true friendship."

We talked a little more along the way and then he dropped me off at home.

"So lil mama when am I gon see you again?"

"Whenever you're free."

"Okay well I call you."

"Okay."

Flight watched me go into the house and then he pulled off. The next morning, I woke up to a ringing phone.

"Hello."

"So how did your date go?" Star asked

"It went good, we had dinner over his friend house. He's a very nice guy and I think that I like him"

"Well someone likes you."

"I know you ain't talking about Juelz!"

"Yes, I am girl when you left he left and everybody knows that Juelz never leaves a party early."

"Well I'm not thinking about him."

"Girl whatever, anyway what you doing today."

"I was waiting for ya'll to tell me."

"Well we going to the movies tonight so call your date because no one can come dateless."

"I'll be sure to call him, what are we going to see."

"I don't know yet we'll figure out when we get there."

"Well okay so what time are we meeting up."

"At nine o'clock."

"Okay see you later."

"Okay."

I got off the phone with star and I called Flight I let him know about the movies and he was all for it.

"So, before we go out to the movies can we have some time together?"

"How would we do that"

"I'll pick you up and we can go out to eat."

"Okay when you're on your way call me."

"Okay."

After getting off the phone with Flight I ate breakfast, showered, brushed my teeth, and then found me something to wear. At twelve thirty Flight called me to let me know that he was on his way. I sprayed some extra perfume on then I was on my way up out the door but not before my mama stopped me.

"Where are you off to?"

"I'm going out to eat with my girls."

"Where are ya'll going?"

"Buffet Bash."

"And how are ya'll supposed to get up there?"

"Terri's mom is taking us."

"Oh okay, well call me and let me know that you're okay."

"Okay ma I will."

I walked out the door and I begin running because I didn't want Flight to get there before I did. When I got there he still hadn't showed, as I got ready to pull out my phone and call him he pulled up.

"Hey lil mama."

"What's up?"

"You."

"That's what's up so where are we going?"

"Where ever you want to go?"

"Well let's go to the Buffet Bash>"

"Let's go."

We made it to the Buffet Bash and we ate pretty much everything and when we were done we paid the tab and left.

"So, what do you want to do next?" Flight asked.

"I don't know."

"Let's go to my place until we go to the movies."

"Okay."

We rode for thirty minutes and we were at his place. He came around the car and opened the car door up for me. We finally reached the porch and he opened the house door for me. When we entered it was a very nice looking place.

"This is nice," I said.

"Thank you."

"So, who did the decorating."

"My mom."

"I could tell that a woman did it."

"How can you tell?"

"Because we're the best decorators in the world."

"Yea okay if it helps you sleep at night."

"And it does."

"Well don't get too excited because I know a little some, some."

"I hear you."

We talked a little more and then we watched television at eight o'clock we left for the movies when we made it there, there was a good number of movies playing but I wanted to see deliver us from evil. When we made it inside we got some snacks and we got settled in our seats. At ten o'clock the movie started and at twelve o'clock the movie was over. After we were done watching the movie we all parted ways and promised to call each other. We pulled off but instead of Flight taking me home he went the opposite way.

"Where we are going?"

"To my place."

"Okay."

"You hesitated a little do you want me to take you home."

"No, I'm okay."

After driving for a while we finally made it to his house.

"May I please use your bathroom?"

"Yea."

He showed me where the bathroom was, when I made it inside I turned the water on and I called my mom.

"Hello."

"Ma the girls and I are just leaving the restaurant and Terri's mom said that she's exhausted so she would like to know if she can bring me home sometime tomorrow morning."

"That's fine but be here before nine because I'm leaving to go out of town and I need to make sure that all is well."

"Okay ma I love you."

"I love you too."

I got off the phone with my mom, turned off the water, and went into the living room.

"Is everything okay?"

"Yea why do you ask?"

"Because you had the water running."

"Oh, I always do that when I have to go I feel more comfortable."

"Ooookay."

"What!"

"Nothing that's just kind of weird."

"Well get used to it."

"I have no choice do I?"

"Not if you want to be with me."

"Well I can dig it, anyway follow me."

We went into his bedroom to lay down and just when I thought that I could go right to bed he begin rubbing all over me. I slid forward to let him know that, that wasn't going to happen but he was so determined that he moved forward too.

"Look Flight there's something I have to tell you."

"What?"

"I'm a virgin."

"Don't worry baby I'll take it slow."

"No, you don't understand!"

"Understand what."

"That I'm waiting."

"Really for what?"

"The right one".

"So, what you're saying is that you don't feel like I'm the right one?"

"No what I'm saying is that I just met you and we don't know each other like that to even think about going that far."

"Well I guess I can't do nothing but respect that."

"Thank you for understanding."

"You welcome."

He rolled over to the opposite side and we both went to bed. The next morning, he took me back to where he picked me up from. I gave him a hug and I waited until he drove off to walk home. When I made it inside my mom was still packing.

"Hey ma."

"Hey baby so did you have fun?"

"Yes, and the food was great."

"That's good but I have to be at the airport by ten-thirty, so listen to my rules carefully, I don't want anyone in my house especially boys, make sure you eat, and make sure that you don't stay out all night."

"Okay ma."

My mom gave me a hug and a kiss and she was out the door. That whole weekend I spent the night over Flight's house. A month had pass and everything with Flight and I was going very well but I hadn't spoken to my friends in a while so I called them so that we could catch up.

"Hello," Terri answered.

"Hey girl what you doing?"

"Nothing Miss busy body."

"I'm so sorry it's just that Flight has been taking me out but I promise to make time for you girls this weekend."

"You better heifer."

"I will."

I got off the phone and I called my other two home girls. After I was done talking to them I hopped in the shower, got dressed, and I was on my way out the door. When I made it to the drive way Terri had already pulled up.

"Hey ya'll," I said as I entered the car.

"Hey," they all said.

"So where have you been Miss Thang," Kiera asked.

"I been around."

"Yea with Flight, you just forgot about us," Star added.

"I'm so sorry ya'll but hey I'm trying to make up for that."

"I guess," Terri said.

"Don't do that, I am trying."

"Well if you trying so much then update us."

"Well everything has been going well, we've been dating for one- month, and I think that I'm even starting to like him."

"Okay that's fine and all but what about the sex?" Star asked.

"Girl we're not having sex we're waiting."

"Girl are you serious, and he still around?" Kiera asked.

"Yes, because my baby loves me."

"Either that or he's gay, crazy, or he's sleeping with someone else," Terri added.

"He's not gay because he wanted to and I let him know that I wasn't ready, he's not crazy, and he's definitely not sleeping with someone else."

"And how do you know that?" Star asked.

"Because I'm always the one holding and answering his calls and texts."

"Oh, shit Miss Ro-Ro got the real deal this time," Kiera said.

"At least I hope so."

Chapter 4

We made it to the restaurant, we found a table, we ordered the food, we ate, and then we talk some more at eleven-thirty Terri dropped me off at home and the first thing I did was call Flight.

"Hello."

"What you doing?"

"Thinking about you."

"Really?"

"Yea I miss you."

"How much?"

"As much as a fat girl miss cake."

"I miss you too."

"That's what's up look baby my homeboy throwing a party tomorrow, so will you do me the honor of being my date."

"Of course, baby what kind of party is it."

"It's his birthday party he's turning twenty."

"Okay but can I bring my girls."

"Baby come on now we suppose to spending time together."

"Baby please, I've spent one month of time with you and I haven't seen my girls in a minute."

"Okay."

"So, what time does it start?"

"At ten o'clock."

"Okay I'll be there."

"Alright."

I hung up the phone and I called and informed my girls about the party. When I hung up with them I showered and went to bed. The next morning, I asked my mom if I could sleep over Star's house and she said that it was okay. I went into my room and I threw me an outfit together after I was done finding everything I called Terri.

"Hello."

"Girl I'm so excited about tonight!"

"Me too I can't wait to find me a fine brotha!"

"You are such a mess."

"Thank you so what are you wearing?"

"I'm wearing a denim skirt, vest, my black halter top, and my black dolce and gabbana shoes."

"Alright miss hot thang!"

"So, what are you wearing?"

"I don't know I'm debating on a dress or some nicely fitted jeans."

"Well you better get it together because time is ticking."

"I know right well, girl I'll hit you up when its time."

"Alright."

I got off the phone with Terri and I heard my mom calling my name. I went down stairs to see what she wanted and I saw a man about six feet tall, brown skin, freshly twisted dreads, slim, and he looked to be somewhere near his forties.

"Ronald this is my daughter Royal, Royal this is my friend Ronald."

"It's a pleasure to meet you Ronald."

"No Royal the pleasure is all mine."

"Royal we're about to go out so if we're not back by the time you leave make sure you lock up the house."

"Okay mama."

I watched my mama grab her purse and I watched Ronald open and close the door for her. After they left I stood there in shock because I couldn't believe that my mom had a new boyfriend. I went into the kitchen and got me something to eat and then I went in the living room to find me something to watch on television. After I was tired of watching television I decided to lock up the house and go for a walk. While walking, I waved at a lot of my neighbors, some that I had never seen and some that I hadn't seen in a while. I walked all the way to the park and I fed the ducks and the geese. I sat there for a while until the sun went down and then I walked back home. When I made it, upstairs I realized that I had left my phone and I had missed calls from my friends and Flight so I called my girls first."

"Hello."

"Hi Kiera what you doing?"

"Nothing everybody getting ready to come over my house and why haven't you been answering your phone we called you like a hundred times."

"I'm sorry I went on a walk and I forgot my phone."

"Yea right Flight probably over there."

"No, he is not."

"Well get ready because after we all get ready we heading your way."

"Okay."

I got off the phone and I called Flight.

"Baby where you at?"

"I just got back from the park."

"Oh, why didn't you answer your phone?"

"Because when I left I forgot to take it."

"Oh, I thought that you had forgot about me."

"No I didn't but I'm about to get ready so I'll see you at the party."

"Alright."

I hung up and then I got in the shower, put on my clothes, and I did my hair and makeup. When I was done, I called my friends to see where they were and they told me that they were ten minutes away. After ten minutes of waiting they pulled up. I got in the car and we pulled off. An hour later we pulled up in front of Flight's house. Everyone got out of the car but not before checking our hair and makeup. When we entered the house, it was crowded, and there was a lot of nice looking brothas. I looked to my left and I saw Flight headed my way.

"Hey ladies."

"Hey," we all greeted.

"Welcome to the party!"

"Thank you," we said.

"So are all these brothas single?" Terri asked.

"Most of them are." Flight responded.

"Well that's our que we'll see ya'll later," Star said and they walked off.

"Well, well, well you looking nice."

"Thank you, you look nice too."

"I'm glad that you notice, come on let me introduce you to some of my friends."

I went over to meet and greet Flight's friends. After meeting, everyone and talking for a while we started dancing and having fun. At eleven forty-five my girls pulled me to the side and told me that they were leaving and they promised to call me in the morning. I hugged them and I watched them leave. When they left, we continued to party. At one o'clock in the morning I got exhausted and I decided I wanted to go to bed. When I made it to the bedroom I saw Flight, his friend and some girl having sex and if that wasn't the worst part they had been sniffing coke.

"What the hell are you doing?"

"Hey baby you want to join us baby you want some coke?"

"No, I don't want to join you and I definitely don't want no coke and you shouldn't be using it either."

I got ready to walk out of the room and he came and grabbed me.

"Come on baby try some it makes the sex better."

"No now get off of me I'm leaving."

"You ain't going nowhere" he said as he grabbed my clothes and ripped my shirt and vest.

"Let me go!"

"Not until you try this good shit."

I pushed him and he slapped the taste out of my mouth so I kicked him in the nuts and I ran out of the house as fast as I could with one shoe on and I didn't stop until I felt like I was far away where he couldn't find me. I thought that, was the worst thing that could ever happen but then it began to rain I walked down the street crying and trying to reach one of my home girls but neither one of them would answer. As I was walking I noticed a car following me and I began running again because I thought that it was either Flight or one of his friends.

"Ms. Royal!" I heard him scream.

I slowed down and I turned around and it was Juelz.

"Do you need a ride?"

"Are you with them?"

"Am I with who?"

"Flight!"

"Na'll."

I got into the suv and he looked me up and down.

"Why you crying Ms. Royal and why your clothes ripped?"

"It's a long story I just need to lay down."

"Look I stay a block away you can spend the night there and I'll drop you off at home in the morning is that okay?"

"Yes, just please get me away from here"

He began driving and just like he said his house was a block away. He got out of the suv came around and opened the door for me and then he unlocked the front door and let me in. He showed me around the house and then he took me to the guest room.

"Are you going to be a'ight?"

"Yea."

"Okay well I'm just in the next room so don't hesitate to call me if you need me."

"Okay."

Chapter 5

I tried to hold myself together but as soon as I heard the bedroom door close I broke down crying all at the same time my phone began to ring and Flight's number showed up and I began to cry even harder I tried my best not to disturb Juelz so I put my face in the pillow.

"I thought I told you to call me if you needed me!"

His voice made me jump.

"I'm fine."

"If you so fine why you crying?"

"It's nothing."

"It's got to be something because if it wasn't you wouldn't be crying, Ms Royal what happened tonight and what happened to your face."

"I don't want to bother you with my problems."

"I asked now tell me."

"Okay, Flight invited me and my friends to one of his friend's house for his homeboy party and I caught him and his friend sniffing coke and running a train on a girl and he wouldn't let me leave and that's how my face and my clothes got like this."

"So, he hit you?" He asked raising his voice. While talking, my phone began to ring and Flights number showed up and Juelz answered it.

"Hello."

"Who is this and where is Royal?"

"So, you can hit a woman but you can't hit a man!"

"Man, fuck you put my girl on the phone!"

"I don't know who your girl is but Ms. Royal is busy right now."

"Nigga when I find out who this is I'ma fuck you up!"

"Don't worry I already know who this is and if you smart you wouldn't want to cross paths with me."

He hung up the phone.

"Let's go clean up your face and find you something to put on."

He took me to the bathroom and he cleaned my face up and then he went to the closet and gave me a pair of his sweats and a t shirt.

"Are you straight in here by yourself?"

"Yes."

He got ready to walk off.

"No can you stay with me/"

"A'ight I'll make a pallet on the floor."

"No I mean sleep in the bed with me."

"Are you sure?"

"Yea."

He slowly walked around and got in the bed and he turned his back towards me. After a while of looking at his back I began rubbing and kissing his back.

"What you doing?" He asked.

"Don't worry I don't have anything I'm a virgin," I said as I began kissing on his back again. He hopped up and looked at me crazy.

"Did I do something wrong?"

"Ms. Royal we can't do this."

"Why not?"

"Because you just going through something right now and I respect you too much."

"You don't like me?"

"That's not the problem I like you but what you holding is special and you need to make sure that when you lose it that it's with the right person because it's not too many girls out there like you."

"But you are a good person."

"Ms. Royal I really do like you but you don't know me and if something is going to happen between us let it happen but don't force it."

"I'm sorry, I'm just so stupid," I said crying.

"You not stupid, it's a'ight just stop crying, look I'll stay and hold you."

He stayed the whole night with his arms wrapped around me. The next morning when I woke up he was gone

I got up and I went down stairs and he was cooking breakfast.

"Are you hungry?"

"Yes."

He fixed my plate and we sat at the table the whole time in silence. After I was done he dropped me off at home.

"Thank you and I'm sorry about last night."

"It's okay Ms. Royal we all have our days."

I got out of the car and I entered the house but my mom still hadn't come home. I went upstairs, looked out the window, and watched Juelz pull off. After he was gone I called my home girls and I told them what happened and although they were angry they were happy that Juelz helped me out after getting off the phone with them I went and took me a hot shower and then I laid down and took me a long nap. When I woke up I had six missed calls five from Flight and one unknown number. So, I called the unknown number back.

"What's up Ms. Royal?"

"How did you get my number?"

"I bumped into one of your friends."

"Which one?"

"A gentleman never tells."

"Well spill the beans then."

"Oh, so you got jokes."

"I'm just messing with you."

"Na'll for real though I was just calling to check on you and to let you know that I'm here if you want to talk."

"Alright I'll definitely keep that in mind."

"That's a bet."

We talked a little more and then we hung up. I went down stairs and my mom had finally made it back.

"Hey baby you had fun last night?"

"Yes, mom it was great!" I lied.

"That's good, what happened to your face?"

"Oh that, Star cat scratched me."

"Oh, that looks bad did you put something on it?"

"Yes ma."

"Okay, you hungry?"

"No I ate already, so how did your date go?"

"It went great; I really do like him."

"Where did ya'll go?"

"We went to a jazz club and then he took me out for dinner. He was a gentleman."

"That's great so when are you going out again"

"Tomorrow but in two weeks he wants me to go to Florida with him."

"Really?"

"Yes, so I'm going shopping for a couple of things today do you want to go with me."

"Yea."

"Well I'm going to take a shower and get dress and then we leaving."

"Okay."

My mom went and took a shower and got dressed and then we left to go to the mall. When we got there, I helped my mom pick out some nice things. It felt nice because my mom and I hadn't done something like this in a long time.

"Do you want something?" My mom asked

"No but let's go to the spa."

"Okay."

We walked through the mall until we found the spa. We got massages, facials, and we took mud baths. It was so relaxing and my mom and I hadn't hung out like this in a long time. We were having so much fun that time was flying by and we didn't even notice.

"Oh, my god it's seven-fifty-nine!"

"What about it?"

"I got to go in early because I got to be at work exactly eight o'clock in the morning."

"Come on you can afford to do one more thing."

"Okay but after this I got to call it a night, so what do you want to do."

"Let's go get something to eat."

We went and found the food court but there were so many restaurants that we were confused but we finally settled with Joe's burger. After we were done with eating just like my mom said she called it a night. When I got in the house I went into my bedroom to watch television until I went to bed. Two weeks had gone by so fast and I stayed in contact with Juelz we had went on plenty of dates but we promised to take it slow because he didn't think that two weeks was enough time for me to get over Flight. While in my Tran of thoughts my phone began ringing.

"Hello."

"Are you busy Ms. Royal?"

"No."

"Can you get out tonight?"

"Yea."

"Well if you ain't dressed already get dressed I'll be there in twenty."

"Alright."

I was already dressed but I got up brushed my teeth, checked my hair, and my makeup. I went into my mom's bedroom.

"Ma?"

"Yea."

"Kiera about to come and pick me up we're all staying over star house is that okay."

"Yea just stay away from that cat."

"Okay."

I went down stairs and every time that I thought I heard a car I looked out of the window. When twenty minutes had passed, I looked out of the window and Juelz was just pulling up. I hurried and went out and locked the door. I walked to his car and he hopped out and came around to open my door.

"Thank you."

"You welcome."

He got inside of the car and we pulled off.

"So where are we going?"

"You'll see."

"I'm not sure if I like the sound of that."

"Don't worry you're going to like it."

He drove for a while and when we stopped we were in front of a very nice house. He got out and then he came and opened my door. I tried to stay a couple feet behind him but he grabbed my hand and he rang the doorbell. When the door swung opened there stood three beautiful little girls with beautiful, curly, sandy brown, hair.

"Uncle J?"

"Why did ya'll open my door and who is it?" I heard a woman asked.

"It's uncle J." one of the little girls said.

The woman came to the door and her face and hair was the same as the three little girls.

"Juelz" she smiled very big and she hugged him.

"Come in don't just stand there," she said.

We walked in and she showed us into the living room. We both went and sat on the sofa.

"Uncle J did you bring us something."

"No, he didn't now take ya'll butts on somewhere, do yawl want something to eat or drink?" she asked.

"No thank you," I responded.

"Bring me some juice," Juelz said.

When she left the room, he pulled out a bag of candy and he gave it to the little girls and put his finger over his mouth letting them know to be quiet. They winked at him and then they ran upstairs. A few seconds later the young lady came around the corner.

"J you better not be giving them candy."

"Come on Portia it's just a little candy."

"Yea your definition for just a little is a bag."

"Yea, yea, yea anyway Portia this is Royal, Royal this is my sister Portia."

"Nice to meet you Royal."

"Nice to meet you too Portia."

"Now I hope my brother has been a good boy because if he hasn't I will slap him for you."

"I'm always a good boy."

"Yea right, so what you been up to?"

"Nothing working."

"Boy hustling is not a job."

"It's bringing in money so it's a job."

"You are so bull headed!"

"Thank you."

The girls came back down stairs smiling and for the first time I realized that they all look the same.

"Are they triplets" I whisper in Juelz ear.

"Yea they triplets, and you don't have to whisper my sister finally overcame it."

"(Laughing) I had no choice."

"You should have seen her when she woke up from having a to be cut they said congratulations Mrs. Rogers you gave birth to triplets."

"I nearly fainted and I almost went into Acoma when they told me that they were all girls."

"So how are you able to tell them apart?" I asked.

"Well, Amanda has blonder hair, Amara is pigeon toed, and amazing has the most amazing blue eyes that I have ever seen in my entire life and besides that I bought them bracelets that they never take off."

"Wow that's amazing!"

"Yea twins and triplets runs in my family" Juelz said

"Yes, they do so you better run for the hills" Portia said.

I began laughing.

"You laughing now but don't say that I didn't warn you." Portia said.

We sat at Portia house for hours just talking and I felt like I had known her forever. After a while we hugged the triplets and Portia and we said our good byes. When we made in the car and he asked.

"Now was that so bad."

"No but next time give me a heads up at least I will be prepared."

"I'll think about it."

Chapter 6

After a while of being in the car I dozed off and when I woke up I was at Juelz house in the guest room. It was hot so I took off my pants and opened the window. The breeze felt so nice. I sat in the window for a while and just smelled the fresh air as I were inhaling all the beautiful nature I nearly chocked from my dry mouth. I got up to get something to drink but not before peeking down the hallway to make sure that the coast was clear and sure enough there was no one in sight so I snuck down the stairs, went into the kitchen, and I got me something to drink.

"You know you shouldn't be sneaking around and your shirt and underwear stealing juice."

"You almost gave me a heart attack where did you come from."

"The theater room."

"Hold up so you have a theater room."

"Yep."

"So, what are you watching?"

"How about you come and find out."

I followed him to the theater room and I couldn't believe how big and beautiful it was.

"So, this is your man cave?"

"Yep."

"So, you watching scar face?"

"I only watch the best."

I sat down in one of the seats and it actually felt like a real movie theater. We finished watching scar face and then he asked.

"So, what do you want to watch next?"

"Oh, you don't have the movie that I want to watch."

"And what's that?"

"Their Eyes Are Watching God."

"Oh well let me go and check"

He left for a few minutes and then he came back and sat right next to me, now I can't lie he had on some nice cologne and he was looking fine as hell. And I had tried to shake it off as much as I could but he was really starting to get next to me.

"Why you looking at me like that?" He asked.

"Oh, I was just admiring your cologne."

"Oh, you like it."

"Yea it smells nice."

"Oh, its polo."

"Oh okay."

When I turned around to the screen the movie had started. We sat and watch the movie and then my favorite part came on.

"That's my favorite part," he said.

"Mines too," I responded.

"Really!"

"Yes, I love it when her and t-cake meet, now that's true love."

He turned around and he started staring at me.

"You're staring," I said without me even turning to look at him.

"I was just admiring your perfume."

"Ha, ha, ha," I said nervously.

He turned his head and started watching the movie and then I started staring at him but before I could turn my head he looked up and I felt butterflies in my stomach. He slowly moved towards me and we began kissing. His lips were so soft and he kissed me so gently and then I felt my area getting wet but before we could move any farther he stopped, stood up, and he left. I was so confused and frustrated. I got up and I went to the guest room but I couldn't sleep so I got up and slowly entered his bedroom. When I got closer he was laying on his back watching me the whole time.

"What you doing?"

"What I want to do."

"We talked about this already."

"I know," I said sitting on top of him.

"And I told you I respect you too much."

"You also said that if something happened between us let it don't force it."

"Yea those was my words but Ms. Royal why do you want to lose your virginity with me?"

"Because I really do like you and when we were just down stairs my body did something that it has never done before."

"I just don't want any regrets."

While he was talking, I began kissing and sucking on his neck.

"Shit, Ms. Royal."

I still wasn't listening I began licking and kissing his chest. I slide his boxers off and I began licking and sucking on his man hood now although I was a virgin I had practiced by myself in my bedroom so when the time came I would know how to do it.

"Fuck," he moaned.

He pulled me up and rolled me over he began kissing on my neck and then I felt that wet feeling again in my area. I made noises that I didn't know that I could make. He slid my shirt off and he began kissing on my chest. He unhooked my bra and he took my breast in his mouth one at a time. It felt so good, I gently grabbed the back of his head. He licked and kissed from my breast to my stomach. He slid my underwear off, spread my legs apart, and he began licking and sucking my wetness.

"Oh, my god!" I screamed as my legs and my body began to shake.

He reached over in the draw and he pulled out a condom and slowly put it on. He went down and tasted my wetness once more before he slowly entered me.

"Ohhhhhh."

"Am I hurting you?" he asked.

"No."

He moved at a slow pace and then when we began to catch a rhythm he rolled me over on top of him. I kept the rhythm that we had and I rode him like I had experience. He then rolled me over on my stomach and he began licking and kissing my back as he entered me again. We went for hours and there was no position that we didn't try. When we were done, he wrapped his arms around me and we both went to sleep. The next morning, I woke up and Juelz was gone, I put on my clothes and I went down stairs and I looked for him but he wasn't there. I sat down and I felt stupid but what did I expect Juelz wasn't going to be trapped with one girl. I mean look at him he could have any girl that he wants. The next thing I heard was a car engine. So, I ran upstairs and I acted like I was fixing the covers. He came into the room.

"Ms. Royal you don't have to do that."

"It's, okay I don't mind."

"Well I do now come on your food is down stairs."

He grabbed my hand and I followed him to the kitchen.

"Which one do you want shrimp fried rice or chicken fried rice?"

"Shrimp."

"Good because chicken is my favorite."

We said our prayer and we began eating but I couldn't take it anymore I just had to say something.

"Look about last night I understand that we just had a moment and its okay if you got a girlfriend, I won't tell her anything."

"Yea I do have a girlfriend and although she's quiet she won't take kindly to you, matter of fact she's here would you like to meet her?"

I wanted to reach across the table and slap the taste out of his mouth.

"Do I have a choice!"

"No."

He took me into the guest bathroom turned on the lights and put me in the mirror.

"Ms. Royal meet my girlfriend Ms Royal," I turned around and playfully hit him in his chest.

"You are such an ass."

"(Laughing) well did you actually think that I brought you around my sister and my nieces just to get that one thing."

"Well you are a ladies' man."

"No I am a lady man, I see those girls out there trying to throw their selves at me all the time but I don't want them, I got who I want.'"

"Yea until I make you mad."

"No until you dump me for another guy and then I still won't leave you alone."

"Oh, a stalker."

"No, I'm not a stalker I just believe in fighting for what's mine, now come on let's go eat our food before it gets cold"

We went and sat down, talked and ate and when we were done he dropped me off at home.

"I'm coming back to pick you up tonight."

"Alright," I kissed him and he came and opened my door so that I could get out.

"Ima, call you a'ight." he said.

"Yea."

I looked back smiled at him and kept walking. Even though he was so nice and he seemed so sincere I was so scared that I would get hurt again but I hoped not. I made it inside the house and I expected my mother to be waiting up for me but she wasn't there. I went into the kitchen and my mother had left a note on the refrigerator.

"If you're reading this letter I have already left to go out of town but I cooked and there's some food in the refrigerator."

I took the sticky note, put it in the trash, and then sat down in front of the television and dozed off. At eleven o'clock in the morning my phone began ringing.

"Hello."

"Girl where have you been we been trying to call you?," Terri said.

"Oh I'm sorry Terri I was with Juelz."

"Oh really what's going on with that?"

"Well we're in a relationship now."

"Ha I knew it!"

"Well if you knew so much how come you didn't know that I lost my virginity last night."

"Well in that case I'm about to pick up the rest of the girls and bitch you got to tell us all the juicy details."

"Okay see you when ya'll get here."

I hung up the phone and I went and took me a shower, I got dressed, did my hair and makeup and then I went down stairs. I looked out the window to see had my home girls made it. Ten minutes later they pulled up. I opened the door and let them in.

"Bitch we here for the details!" Star said.

"Well hey to ya'll too."

"We sorry girl hey now get to the details," Kiera said.

We sat down in the living room and I told them everything that happened and they were so happy for me.

"Now that's a good man," Kiera said.

"You said that with Flight and look how that turned out," I said.

"Well I actually agree with Kiera this time" Star said

"Yea me too baby girl you just got to let your guard down before you miss out on a good man," Terri said.

"I guess I'll try it but if something goes wrong I'm blaming it on all of ya'll."

"We accept that challenge," they all said.

"So when is the next time ya'll going to see each other?" Terri asked.

"Tonight."

"I'm so happy for you." she said.

"Well at least one of us is happy" Star said

"Well you should be happy too because Cedrick is a nice guy," I said.

"Well he kind of came in and caught me cheating on him with my ex."

"Star!," Kiera said.

"Well I can't help it Cedrick just wasn't putting it down like my ex."

"Now that just sad," Terri said.

We continued to talk for a while. Then I warmed up the food that my mom had cooked. I split it between all four of us, we ate and watched television. At eight-forty-five they all left and I called Juelz.

"Hello."

"Hi."

"Ms. Royal."

"How did you know I blocked my number?"

"Because you're the only girl that I'm talking to and I know that sweet sexy voice anywhere."

"Oh really?"

"Yep so are you ready?"

"Yea."

"Okay I'm on my way."

"Okay."

I got off the phone, I checked my hair, and my makeup. After I was done I waited for him to come. While I waited I watched television. After ten minutes I heard the doorbell so I went to answer it.

"Flight what are you doing here?"

"Why haven't you been answering my phone calls?"

"Because we're done, it's over!"

"And what nigga you had answering your phone?"

"My nigga now, get out of my door way!"

"I ain't going nowhere."

And it was as if he heard my cry for help because as I was struggling to get Flight out of my door way Juelz pulled up and hopped out of the truck.

"Ms. Royal do we have a problem?"

"Naw man I'm just talking to my girl," Flight said

"Naw bro you just talking to my Girl!"

"Ahh man no disrespect she just hadn't called me and I was trying to see what's up that's all I don't want no problems."

"She ain't answering your calls because she answering mine so if you don't want no problems you better leave."

"Okay man I want mess with her no more."

"Bet."

He didn't walk but he ran and got in his car and left.

"You a'ight."

"Yea."

"Why you open the door for him?"

"Because I thought it was you."

"See Ms. Royal you gotta start using the peep hole."

"I know that now."

"You ready?"

"Yea just let me get the key so I can lock up the house."

I went and got the key and I locked the door then we got inside the car and we pulled off but my conscience was urging to know.

"Can you tell me something?"

"Anything you want to know Ms. Royal."

"Why was Flight so afraid of you?"

He looked at me and smiled and then he said, "I don't know."

"You just said anything I want to know."

"I know but…"

"So we holding secrets now."

"Not secrets but a secret yes."

"Okay so that means that I can hold one secret?"

He gave me a crazy look.

"Don't look at me like that, I don't know if I'm in the car with a murderer or what."

"Come on Ms. Royal don't act like that."

"Okay."

We rode a little while longer before making it to his place and I didn't even wait for him to open my door I just got out of the car, closed the door, and waited in front of the door until he unlocked it. And when he did I went straight to the guest room and lied down.

"Why you in here?" he asked

"Because I'm a guest."

"How are you a guest?"

"Because you are a stranger."

"Stop acting like that Ms. Royal."

"Goodnight."

"You can't go to sleep somebody coming over to meet you."

"Well just tell them you wouldn't be honest with me so I went to bed."

"A'ight I'll be real with you but first you got to make me a promise."

"And what's that?"

"That you won't look at me different."

"Okay I promise."

"When I was little my daddy run the streets, I mean didn't nothing go on without him knowing and if it did they paid the price. One day my dad heard about a drop that supposed to been happening and it had something to do with some people that was a part his crew, so he felt disrespected. He knew the time and the place where the drop supposed to been happening. So he showed up but it was a set up by this slimy nigga name psycho from my dad crew anyway when he got there they shot my dad two times in the head, ten times in the chest and once in the leg. Now from him doing that he would move up in a higher position but what they didn't know is that his fourteen-year-old son was there and that he had seen the whole thing. So I ran to my dad's hang out spot and I told his crew what I had saw. The first thing my dad's best friend wanted to do was retaliate but my uncle told him that he had a plan. When psycho arrived one of my dad's friends left to get his body. Psycho was so nervous but he tried to act cool but he messed up when he asked had they seen my dad that day. My uncle played it cool so he said that he hadn't but my uncle lied and said that the night before he had spoken to my father about a drop they had to make and he ask psycho to come with him. psycho went and the rest of the crew followed they pulled up at a garage and everybody entered including psycho that's when they closed the door and turned on the lights and my dad's body was laying on the back of his friend truck then psycho tried to play dumb and asked what happen to buck that's what they called my dad. That's when everybody grabbed him, tied him up, beat him until he started talking, and killed him. They set something up to catch the rest of the guys and I had to kill the one that killed my dad. After that my uncle taught me everything that I needed to know about the game to survive in the street when I turned eighteen I took my dad's place and I been in the streets every since".

"So you're in a gang?"

"Naw I'm in a crew and that name speaks volumes."

"You think your dad would have wanted you to live like this."

"I don't know but it's too late now."

"It's never too late."

"See that's why I didn't want to tell you."

"Okay I'll stop talking about it, but first you gotta make me a promise like I made you a promise."

"And what's that?"

"Promise me that you'll always come home in one piece."

"Awww Ms. Royal going to miss me."

"I'm serious Juelz; I didn't start dating you and catching feeling for you for me to end up at a funeral."

"A'ight Ms. Royal I Promise" he said as he kissed me. We were on our way down the stairs when someone rang the doorbell. Juelz answered the door and there stood a lady that looked no older than forty. Juelz helped her in the house and then he introduced us.

"Mama this is my girlfriend Royal, Royal this is my mother Marie."

"Nice to meet you Ms. Marie."

"Nice to meet you too Royal, but do me a favor just call me Marie or mama because that Ms. makes me feel old."

"Oh I'm sorry."

"(Laughing) don't take it personal honey that just means that your parents raised you to have respect but I just turned twenty-five."

"Okay well that mean that you not the lady that I was looking for because my mama just turned forty-five," Juelz said.

"No twenty-five you have it all wrong," I said.

"Exactly, he just mad because I'm still young."

"Okay ma you still young, so have you ate."

"No."

"What do you want to eat?"

"What do you have to cook I'll cook it."

"Ma you already know that I don't want you in the kitchen you do that enough at home but when you're at my house you sit down while I cater to you so what do you want to eat."

"I'll take some homemade spaghetti."

"Alright ma I'm about to cook."

"I'll cook it," I said.

"Now child you just sit on down, you company too."

"No really I don't mind."

"Don't worry Ms. Royal I got it."

"Why you don't trust my cooking?" I asked

"Don't do that Ms. Royal!"

"Well."

"A'ight you got it but at least let me help."

"Okay."

Chapter 7

We made it into the kitchen and I started with the pasta when the pasta was almost done I started with the ground beef. When I was sure that my pasta and my ground beef was ready I drained them, mixed them together, and added the sauce, salt, and pepper. When it was done I took the garlic bread out of the oven and I served the food. We sat at the table and we laughed and talked. After dinner Juelz cleared the table and cleaned the dishes and that left his mom and me talking.

"So how long have you and Juelz been dating?"

"For about two weeks."

"And he's already introducing you to the family."

"Is that a bad thing?" I asked worried

"No that means that he really likes you and with that maybe you can convince him to get out of the street because I'm concern about him."

"I'll try but your son is very bull headed."

"Oh but don't I know it."

His mom and I talked a little more before we called it a night and Juelz showed her to the guest room.

The next morning Marie left to go visit Portia and then she would be on her way back to California. That same morning Juelz dropped me off at Kiera's house.

"What time do you want me to come and pick you up?" Juelz asked.

"I'll call you."

"Bet."

I gave him a kiss and I got out of the car. When I approached the door to knock Kiera had already opened it.

"Girl how did you know that I was here.?"

"Because I smelled you from a mile away."

"Ha, ha, ha very funny."

"Well you asked that crazy question."

"So where the rest of the crew are they coming because Terri said that she got to show us something.

"What is it?"

"I don't even know yet."

We waited for about an hour and then Star and Terri showed up.

"Hey ya'll," I said.

"Hey," they responded.

"So what was so important that we all had to meet up at my house?" Kiera asked.

"I was with John last night and while he was taking a shower I took the liberty to go through his bag, when I say that I found hard, soft, mid, loud, and guns girls I hit the jack pot."

She pulled out the duffel bag and showed it to us.

"Terri ain't he gon come looking for his stuff?" I asked.

"Yes of course but by that time I'm gon be long gone."

"Girl this is very dangerous you playing with fire," Star said.

"Yea I agree with Star," Kiera said.

"Well he doesn't know where I stay so all I got to do is stay low."

"Well for him to have all this shit that means he got connections and that also means that you better watch your back because he won't be the only one looking for you," Star said.

"Yea and like my mama always said you play with fire and you will get burned," I said.

"Yea and what you need all this stuff for, I mean our parents have money so we're well taken care of," Kiera said.

"Yea but that's our parent's money, but if we make our own money it's going to be a lot of things that change, I mean come on soon we're all going to be eighteen, we're going to be off to college and eventually we're gon want to move into our own place and then mama and daddy ain't gon pay your rent or bills. I'm just saying wouldn't ya'll like to be prepared before you step out into the real world, I mean come on we have always been given something out of a silver spoon and I don't want to go from that to being poor now ya'll know I'm right," Terri said.

"Well ya'll she is kind of right," Star said.

"Yea," Kiera said.

"I understand where you coming from but why can't we just make money the honest way," I said.

"You really think working for minimum wage is going to get you to where you are trying to go/" Terri asked.

"I don't know but how can I preach to Juelz about being in the street if I'm doing the same thing."

"What Juelz don't know won't hurt him."

"But what if he finds out I'll be jeopardizing a good relationship?"

"Well like you said if he leaves then he wasn't the right one anyway."

"I wasn't talking about this type of situation; I mean think about who all we could be putting into danger."

"Ro-Ro I promise you that we gon sell this stuff and then we gon get out it's a onetime deal."

"But we don't even know how much to sell this stuff for."

"I got my connections, look this stuff have to be worth thousands of dollars."

"Look I don't know I'll have to think about it."

"Well I'm in," Star said.

"Me too," Kiera said.

I shook my head and I called Juelz this was something big and I didn't know which way to turn I mean it was a good deal and all but it was also dangerous and I wasn't ready to risk my life all over some fast money. Thirty minutes had passed and Juelz finally pulled up. When I got into the car Juelz sensed something wrong.

"What's wrong Ms. Royal."

"Nothing."

"You sure because you look upset."

"I'm okay it's nothing really I just need to relax."

"Well that's good because I got a great day planned for us."

"Like what!" I asked excitingly.

"You'll see."

We drove around a while and then we stopped at a park.

"Why are we here?" I asked

He got out of the car, came around to my side, let me out, went into the back of his suv, and pulled out a blanket and a basket.

"We're having a picnic."

"This is romantic I never thought of you as a romantic type of guy."

"They say love makes you do foolish things."

We went and we sat close to the pond he put the blanket down, then the basket, and then champagne. I sat down on one end and he sat down on the other. He opened the basket and he pulled out two plates.

"Now normally when you go on a picnic they have sandwiches and fruit but seeing that I'm not like other people I made crab salad, shrimp and fish."

"Awww that's so sweet," I said leaning over to give him a kiss.

"Only for my lady."

"Oh don't worry because my man will get a reward for this."

"Oh really."

"Yep."

We ate, talked and then we made love in the park. We went from there to Juelz house and we made love again.

"Baby are you asleep?" Juelz asked.

"No I'm just thinking."

"Thinking about what."

"Thinking about the fact that my mom is coming back tomorrow and our time will be cut short."

"So why don't you tell her the truth?"

"Because my mom is kind of, like you and everything is either her way or no way at all."

"But you're going to be eighteen in two weeks."

"I know but I just need some more time."

"Are you embarrassed by me?"

"No Juelz I just don't want to hear her long speech about what she worked her fingers to the bone for, look baby I'm going to tell her I promise just give me time."

"A'ight."

While we were in the middle of our conversation Juelz phone began to ring.

"Hello."

"Yea I got that."

"A'ight I'll be there in thirty."

He got off the phone and looked at me.

"And just where you will be in thirty."

"I got a drop to make."

"And that gives you the right to leave me in this bed all alone."

"Baby I'ma be back."

"And how do you know that I will even be here when you get back."

"I trust my instincts."

"Well, guess what your instincts is going to leave you with an empty bed by the time you return."

"Come on Ms. Royal why you acting like that."

I rolled over and turned my back towards him. He came to the other side of the bed kissing my neck.

"Ms. Royal."

"What?"

"Come on baby."

"Are you sure you're not going to meet up with a girl?"

"Ms. Royal come on you know me better than that the only girl I see is you."

"Yea it better be."

"So does that mean that I can go?"

"Go ahead."

"And will you be here when I get back?"

"I guess."

"You better be," he said kissing me.

He put his clothes and shoes on and he got in the car and left. I just laid there thinking about what Terri had said until I dozed off. An hour later I was awakened by Juelz wrapping his arms around me.

"Why did it take you so long?"

"Because it takes me thirty minutes to get there and thirty minutes to get back."

"Yea okay."

He rolled me over and began kissing on my neck.

"Come on Juelz I'm tired."

"Are you sure?" He asked sucking on my breast.

"Ohhhhhh Juelz," I managed to say as he slid my underwear off and taste my wetness he did it until I climaxed and my legs and my body began to shake. He rolled on a condom and he entered my wetness stroking very slowly. It felt so good that I felt like I had walked out of my body. He sat up on the edge of the bed while I rode his man hood and I urged him to go deeper. We made love for hours like we were trying to start a fire and when we both climaxed it felt like the earth shook. After we were done we both rolled over and went to sleep. The next morning Juelz dropped me off at home. I got in the shower, found me something to put on, and waited for my mom to arrive. At eleven o'clock am my mom finally showed up.

"Hey ma."

"Hey, come help me with my bags.

I helped her take her bags upstairs.

"So how was your little vacation?" I asked.

"It was great I mean we went to so many different areas and the beach was so beautiful."

"Do you have any pictures?"

"Yea, so what did you do while I was gone?"

"The same thing I do while you're here hang out with my girls."

"Well I have a surprise for you."

"Really?"

"Yes but you have to wait for your birthday."

"Ma!"

"Don't ma me you can wait."

"I guess."

"Well I'm a little tired so I'm going to take a shower and then I'm taking a nap."

"Okay."

"So what you doing today?"

"Nothing but meeting up with my crew."

"Okay well be careful!"

"I will."

I called Terri and we all met up at Star house.

"So what happen with you and Juelz last night?" Star asked.

"Well we went to the park, had a picnic, and we made love by the pond."

"That sounds so romantic," Kiera said.

"It was, he surprised me with that."

"Well enough about that, so did you think about what we talked about?" Terri asked.

"Dang what got your panties in a bunch?" Star asked.

"Nothing but what ya'll talking about is irrelevant and I'm trying to make some money."

"Well, Ms. Thang FYI my relationship is not irrelevant it's very relevant to me and yes I did think about what we talked about and since you're so thrilled about making money did it ever accrue to you that even if we don't get killed that we can end up doing some serious time in jail for this?" I asked

"Ro-Ro I didn't mean it like that, all I'm saying is that we can make fortunes off of this stuff. And yes I did think about the jail time and that's why we gon rent my cousin apartment for a little while," Terri said.

"Well look I'm in but if I feel that it's getting too dangerous then I'm backing out, deal?" I asked.

"Deal!," Terri said.

We sat and talked about how much we would sell each product for, our connections, and how we would get people to start buying. After hours of talking we felt like it was time to call it a night if we were going to get up and start in the morning because as the saying goes the early bird catches the worm. When I got home I took a shower and I called Juelz after we were done talking I went to sleep. The next morning, I woke up, took a shower, got dressed, ate, and waited for Terri to arrive.

"So what are you girls doing today?" My mom asked

"We just hanging out at the mall."

"Oh do you need some money?"

"No I been saving money up when you give it to me."

"Oh okay so what time should I expect you to be back."

"I don't know."

"Well it better not be late."

"Ma I'm seventeen."

"And you're still living under my roof."

"Wow alright I'll be sure to come back at a good time."

An hour later Terri showed up and we went to her cousin's apartment. When we got there, there was a man waiting for Terri outside of the door. Terri unlocked the door, let everyone in, and then she introduced everyone to the strange man.

"Everyone this is Trip, my connection."

"Hey Trip," we all said.

"Hey ladies," he spoke back.

"So where should we start?" Terri asked.

"Well first we need to start bagging everything but first how many pounds of weed you got." Trip asked.

"I got five pounds," Terri answered.

"Well you can get at least $1000 for each pound." Trip said.

"Shit that's $5,000 just for the weed."

"Yea a kilo of that hard will get you at least $36,000."

"Now we talking," Star said.

Trip showed us how to cook our products, how to chop our products, how to weigh our products, how to bag our products, how much to sell our products, and who to sell it to. I sat and I took everything in now I didn't know this Trip cat but if Terri trusted him then I guess I had no choice but to do the same but I was going to keep my eyes and ears open because I refuse to be sleep with my eyes open. Trip showed us some people that we could sell to and get the word out. We went from selling $10 bags to selling $150 8balls. The word had got out so fast that at the end of the week I had already stacked up on $17,350. That was a lot of money for a beginner but the deal was for us to get in and get out. The next week my mom told me that since my birthday was coming up that I could have a party. I was so busy juggling getting my party together and getting at least four Hours making money. So that week I brought home $4,200 but $21,550 wasn't bad for someone that had just got into the game and got out. That Friday when I got home I found me an outfit that I would wear for my birthday. I had got all the decoration and I was set. After I put all my things together I called my girls.

"Hello."

"What's up Terri?"

"Girl this money, look I know that I said that we would get in and get out but after I seen how much money I made in two weeks I couldn't resist so I went and got some more stuff to sell and this time it's not stolen so are you in or out?" She asked.

"Naw I'm out I mean the money is good and all but it was starting to get too dangerous for me."

"How you figure?"

"Terri ya'll got robbed at gun point!"

"But that didn't stop shit because we went right back out there and made double of what we got robbed for."

"Look I respect the fact that you trying to make money but I'm out."

"Well if at any time you want to come back you know that you can."

"Naw I'm good but ya'll be safe."

"We will."

"Oh by the way are ya'll coming to my party tomorrow."

"Ro-Ro girl you know we got to show up and show out, so what time is it starting."

"At nine"

"Okay we'll be there."

"Alright."

I got off the phone with Terri and I called Juelz.

"Ms. Royals."

"Hey what you doing?"

"Making a drop."

"So are you stopping by tomorrow."

"What you doing?"

"I'm having a party."

"Yea you know I got to stop by and show my lady some love."

"Okay that's what's up."

"So I haven't been seeing you lately what's up."

"I just had my hands full trying to make sure that my party is perfect but all of that will be over with after tomorrow."

"I hope so because you got a lot of making up to do."

"Oh trust me that won't be a problem but I got to get up early in the morning to go pick up my cake and stuff so I'll talk tomorrow."

"A'ight bet."

I got off the phone with Juelz, took a shower and went to bed. The next morning, I was awakened by my mom singing.

"Happy birthday to you, happy birthday to you, happy birthday to you, happy birthday to you.

"Thanks ma."

"You welcome I figure since it's your eighteenth birthday and you turned into a young lady that I could serve you breakfast in bed."

"Awww ma why are you crying?"

"Because you're not a baby anymore."

"But I'm gon always be your baby."

"And you better know it now hurry up and eat breakfast so that you can get ready to go pick up your cake."

"Alright ma."

Chapter 8

I ate breakfast, put on some clothes, and I went and picked my cake up. After that I went to the store, got some ice cream, and made it back to the house so that my girls could help me decorate. We decorated the house, cooked the food, and made sure that everything was in place. By the time we finished it was five o'clock I hurried and jumped in the shower and got dressed for the party, at six-thirty everyone started to arrive but there was one person that I was looking for that hadn't quite made it. It felt like hours when it was only thirty minutes extra when he finally arrived. When he entered the door he looked across the room at me. I could see him looking but I pretended that I was so into my girls' conversation that I wasn't paying any attention. After a couple of minutes, he finally walked over.

"Hi ladies."

"Hello," we all chanted.

"I don't mean to be rude but can I borrow your friend for just one second?" he asked.

"Of course," they said.

He pulled me to the side.

"Happy birthday Ms. Royal."

"Thank you but is that all I get?"

"Be patient I got you."

"Okay but since you here let me introduce you to my mom."

"Hold up you sure you want to do that now?"

"So when do you think would be a great time?"

"How about after the party when everyone is gone because it's your day and I don't want it to go wrong."

"Okay."

"So since we here Ms. Royal can I have the first dance?"

"Of course."

He pulled me to the dance floor and we danced to two slow songs, it felt so nice and he actually made me feel Royal. We danced until our feet were tired and afterwards he went and got us something to drink. We all sat around talking, laughing, eating, and dancing. At two o'clock am everyone song happy birthday, I made a wish and I blew out the candles. When everyone was done I started to receive presents.

"Okay so I know that I have been a very over protective mother but that's because I love you and I would do anything to keep you safe and I know that you have never really been anywhere major so I bought four tickets for you and your home girls to go to California tomorrow so you can finish celebrating your eighteenth birthday," my mom said.

"Aww thanks ma."

"You welcome."

"Well we weren't sure what to get you because you pretty much have everything but we did notice that we have never seen you with any Jewelry on so I bought the necklace, Star bought the bracelet, and Kiera bought the ring and just to inform you their all eighteen carrot gold," Terri said.

"Awww thanks girls that so sweet."

"You welcome," they said.

"Well I don't know how I'm going to top all of this, well actually I do. Ya'll know that I had to do something very special for Ms. Royal so everyone follow me please," Juelz said.

We all followed him outside.

"Now this might be a bit much but I'm willing to do that just for you so here's your new Lamborghini Huracan LP 610-4 and here's the keys to go with it."

"Oh my god, thank you so much!" I screamed jumping up and down hugging him.

"You welcome," Juelz said.

After I had opened all of my presents we danced a little more and at three o'clock am the party was over. My girls and Juelz stayed behind and helped my mom and I clean up and when it was clean everyone left with the exception of Juelz. I knew why he had stayed behind but now I was starting to get a bit nervous but I couldn't let that happen because if I did we might as well go our own separate way because we would always be a secret.

"So are you ready?" I asked Juelz.

"It's either now are never."

"Okay let's go."

I took Juelz in the living room where my mom had begun watching television.

"Ma I want you to meet somebody."

"Okay have a seat," she said.

We sat down on the opposite sofa from my mom.

"Ma this is Juelz, my boyfriend, Juelz this is my mama Paris."

"How you doing?" Juelz asked.

"And how long have you two been dating?" she asked Juelz ignoring his question on purpose.

"Almost a month." he responded.

"So where do you work?"

"I'm not working right now."

"So let me get this straight, you don't have a job but you can afford to buy my daughter a very expensive car.

"No and yes."

"So let me just be blunt I don't know what your intentions are with my daughter but she's going to college next year and I don't think you fit the ideal man that my daughter needs to accomplish her dream."

"Well, Ms. Wilkinson no disrespect but I care about your daughter a great deal and as long as I'm supporting her 100% and pushing her to accomplish her dream it doesn't matter what life style I'm living because at the end of the day just like you want the best for her so do I."

"Well maybe I'm not being clear I don't want my daughter to see you anymore so you can get those keys and take your very expensive car back with you."

"Ma!"

"Don't ma me I didn't work my fingers to the bone for you to date a drug dealer!"

"Ma I'm eighteen years old now you can't tell me who I can and can't date."

"Although you just turned eighteen you still living under my roof and you will go by my rules and I said you can't date him anymore and that's final."

"No disrespect but I didn't come to start any problems I simply expressed how I feel about your daughter through the present I bought for her and I understand how you feel about your daughter and I'm not trying to come between you and your daughter relationship but what you need to understand is not everyone was born with a silver spoon in they mouth and so I got out there and got it the best way I knew how."

"That's no excuse you could have done anything you wanted to but this the life you chose so don't come around here with that sorry excuse."

"Look I didn't come here to start any problems but I love your daughter and we are going to be together."

"If she continues to see you she will not be living under my roof."

"That's fine she can come live with me."

"Oh really, so Royal what are you going to do?" my mom asked.

"Yea Ms. Royal what are going to do?"

I was so confused I didn't know what I wanted to do I mean my mom was being unreasonable and I did love Juelz but I wasn't sure if I was willing to take a big step like moving in with him I mean what would happen if he decided he was done with me where would I go and the worst part was that I was being asked to choose.

"Royal!" my mom yelled.

"Ms. Royal what you gon do?"

"I......I......I don't know."

"Well you better choose wisely," my mom said.

"You know what since you can't choose I'll choose for you I'm out call me when you old enough to make your own decision."

"Juelz!"

I screamed but he wasn't listening he got the keys for the car that he had just got me he let his friend drive his car while he drove mines. I stood in the door crying hoping that he would change his mind and hoping that he would turn around but he didn't.

"Thanks a lot you just destroyed a good relationship."

"Girl I'm trying to protect you!"

"I don't need you to protect me!"

"What you mean you don't need me to protect you, you just turned eighteen and you think you grown but age don't make you grown actions do."

"Well I guess you are a child because your actions were very childish!"

"Little girl you better watch your mouth!"

"See that's your problem now, I'm not a little girl, I don't need you to protect me from the world, I don't need you trying to live my life for me, I need space to grow, sooner or later I'm going to step out into the real world and you're not going to be there to protect me, that right there is called life and you need to get used to it."

"I'll get used to it when you start paying bills or better yet when you move out of my house."

"I'm glad that I know your true feelings, oh and f. y. I, I don't know if I even want to go to college!"

I stormed off and I went into my room and called Star.

"Hey birthday girl what you doing?"

"I think Juelz broke up with me."

"What, what happen?"

"My mom didn't agree with me dating him and they wanted me to choose and if I chose him I had to move out and although he said that I can move with him that's a big move."

"Wow, well do you want me to come over?"

"No I'll just see ya'll tomorrow when we leave for the trip."

"Okay well I hope you feel better."

"Thanks."

I got off the phone with star, packed my clothes, showered, and cried myself to sleep. The next morning, I woke up, showered, got dressed, put my hair in a ponytail, and waited until Terri came to pick me up to leave for the trip. While sitting on my bed I wondered what Juelz was doing. I wanted to call him but he was probably too upset with me. While in a daze my mom came into my bedroom and sat down.

"I thought that we should talk before you leave for your trip."

"About?"

"Look I know that you feel that the world is coming to an end but trust me when I say you're young and you have all the time in the world to date and when you find that right guy you will forget all about that boy."

"And how do you know?"

"Because I've been young, I've dated, and I've been with guys like him and they had no goals and they only wanted one thing."

"Well, Juelz is different."

"No he's not."

"You don't know you never even tried to get to know him."

"Because you don't need that kind of guy in your life."

"Mom I understand that how he makes his money is not good but behind all of that is a very nice guy that I fell in love with."

"You're young right now you don't know what love is."

"I'm young but I have a heart just like you do, I feel just like you do, I know that my heart skips a beat when I'm around him, I know that my palms get sweaty, I know that I lose my breath when he kisses me, I know that when we make love that he's making love to my mind, body, and soul, and I know that without him that my heart completely stops beating."

"Royal you're having sex!"

"Yes."

"Why didn't you let me know that you felt like you were ready to have sex?"

"Because I knew that you wouldn't approve of the guy that I wanted to lose my virginity with."

"That's because he's not worth your time."

While talking to my mom Terri pulled up and blew her horn.

"Well, mom I would really like to continue this obnoxious conversation but that's my cue to leave."

I grabbed my suit case, my purse, went outside, hopped in the car, and we pulled off. A little after being on the road Terri began talking.

"Ro-Ro I heard about what happened and I'm sorry but I'm here if you want to talk."

"Yea that was wrong what your mom did," Kiera added.

"Yea we your sisters we're going to always be here for you," Star said,

"Thanks ya'll," I said.

"So have you talked to him yet?" Terri asked.

"No because he might be upset with me"

"Well you did kind of choose your mom over him," Star said.

"Yea and you are still going on a trip after what happened instead of calling him and explaining," Kiera added.

"I know but that's a big leap moving in with someone I mean what if everything goes wrong then I have to come crawling back home to my mother all humiliated and that's only if she decides to let me come back and as far as calling him I just don't know what to say."

"That is a big leap but you're taking a chance with love," Star said.

"Well I don't know I just need to go on this trip so that I can get my thoughts together."

"Look I understand that but Juelz is a good man and he loves you and while you're on this trip getting your thoughts together some hoochie can be all over your man," Terri said.

"Well if it's that easy for him to get over me then we weren't met to be after all."

I wanted so badly to get off of this conversation so I laid back and closed my eyes. When we made it to the airport we put our suit cases on the scanner and we went through the metal detector. After we had been checked we boarded the plane. When I got on the plane I just laid back and tried to get my mind off of Juelz but it was becoming very difficult. It took us four and a half hours to make it to California. When we got off of the plane we went through baggage claim to get our bags and then we caught a cab to the hotel. After checking in instead of going out to see the view I decided to take me a much needed nap but it actually ended up being the next morning.

"Okay girls so since someone went to sleep on us yesterday what's the first thing we're going to do together" Star said

"How about the beach," Kiera suggested.

"Yea that sounds great," Terri said.

"Well, you guys go on without me I'm still a little tired," I said.

"No, no, no, now I know that you're sad and I feel for you but I will not have one of my best friends moping around the whole trip, I mean come on Royal this is supposed to be fun and besides you're not acting like the fun Ro-Ro that I know," Star said.

"I'm sorry ya'll I'm just not feeling this," I said.

"Look we understand all your hurt and pain but we promise you that if you try to make the best out of this trip that we'll do anything to get you and Juelz on track but please Ro-Ro at least take this opportunity to get a break from all the craziness at home," Kiera said.

"Okay I'll try."

Chapter 9

We stayed in California for a week going to different beaches, seeing all the sights, enjoying the spa, and enjoying the great room service and when it was time to return back home I felt like I was moving to a new home. The trip was very much needed but the sad part now was that I had to step back into reality. We took the four-and-a-half-hour flight back home. We went through baggage claim to get our items and Terri drove us home. When I made it inside my mom was at work. I went into my room unpacked my bag, took me a hot bubble bath, got dressed, and took a nap. For what seemed like hours was only an hour of rest. I got up and went down stairs to get me something to eat and to sit in front of the television. While watching the television my phone began ringing.

"Hello."

"Are you ready to face your fears?" Star asked.

"I don't know."

"Well you better figure it out real fast because I'm outside of your door."

"Star!"

"Don't Star me bring your butt on so we can get this over with!"

I put my shoes on, locked the door, and went and hopped into the car.

"Now what if this goes bad?"

"Well you just suck it up and keeps it moving."

"Easier said than done."

"I know but you never let a man see you break."

It felt like hours but it only took us thirty minutes to get there and at least ten minutes to get me out of the car.

"Do you want me to sit out here?"

"Please."

"I'll be waiting for you."

"Okay."

I began walking to the door and just as I was about to ring the doorbell the door swung open and out came a light skin girl about five-six with shoulder length hair. Juelz looked up and he saw me.

"Ms. Royal."

I turned around and ran back to the car and we drove off. I felt so stupid how I could have let myself get so wrapped up around this boy he was no different than Flight. I began crying. My phone began ringing and when I looked it was Juelz calling but I ignored it.

"Are you okay ?" Star asked

"Yea I'll be fine."

Star dropped me off at home and I went straight to my bedroom. Everything was going downhill and I felt like an idiot. I cried so hard. Later on that night I was awaken by my mom.

"How was your trip?"

"It was nice."

"See I told you that you would have fun you'll forget all about that no good boy."

"Yea."

She gave me a hug, a kiss, and she left the room. I went back to sleep. The next morning, I woke up and took a shower, got dressed, and I went down stairs to get me something to eat. When I made it in the kitchen my mom had left a sticky note letting me know that my food was in the microwave. I warmed my food and I went and sat in front of the television. As soon as I got ready to eat my phone began ringing.

"Hello."

"Hey Ro-Ro I heard about what happened," Terri said.

"Yea."

"Do you want us to come over and keep you company?"

"Naw I'm good."

While talking on the phone someone started ringing the doorbell I don't know why I didn't look through the peephole I just opened the door.

"Hey Terri can I call you back?"

"Yea is everything okay?"

"Yea."

I got off the phone with Terri.

"Juelz what are you doing here?"

"You didn't see what you thought you saw."

"Oh so I didn't see a girl coming out of your house?"

"No, Yes."

"So I did see what I thought I saw?"

"Look the girl wasn't there for me."

"It's okay you don't have to lie to me, I couldn't make up my mind so you went to find someone that could."

"That's not true."

"Then what's the truth then?"

"That was my home boy's girl they had a disagreement and she tried to get him to come back home."

"Do you really expect me to believe that?"

"Would you like for me to call him or better yet would you like to go by his house because I have no reason to lie."

"But I saw."

"Nothing you just assumed."

"I'm sorry."

"It's a'ight so how was your vacation?"

"Miserable."

"My week was too, because I couldn't seem to get you off of my mind."

"I couldn't stop thinking about you either, I started to call but I thought that you were mad at me."

"I wasn't mad at you I just felt like you needed time."

"I did, I mean I was scared about how things might go if I was to move in with you and I'm still a little afraid but I don't want to stop seeing you."

"So how do you expect for us to keep seeing each other until you make up your mind?"

"I'll do what I did when we first met."

"What sneak behind your mom back?"

"Yea, we don't have a choice."

"We do have a choice."

"Look I just don't want to make a huge mistake, so I kind of want to slow things down."

"I can't do nothing but respect that."

"Are you angry with me?"

"Naw I'm good but I got a couple of things that I got to do so I'll hit you up later."

I gave him a kiss on the lip but the kiss felt different it wasn't as passionate as I remembered and I really didn't know where we would go from here. But I did feel like everything would work itself out. A month had passed since then and we were still sneaking around seeing each other and honestly I felt like it was getting old. I was eighteen years old and I still had to lie about who I dated. While my friends were enjoying their love life I was hiding mine and I just couldn't do it anymore, so something had to give but for now I had to put that on the back burner because I was receiving letters from colleges from left and right I still hadn't made up my mind if I was going or not. While sitting in my room thinking my phone started to ring.

"What's up Terri Girl?"

"(Crying) Royal."

"What's wrong?"

"Kiera and Star got robbed, they were raped, and stabbed their, at the hospital we have to get down there now."

"What?"

"I'm so sorry."

"Oh my god NOOOOO!"

I dropped the phone and I fell to the floor. Somehow I managed to call Juelz. Thirty minutes later he came to pick me up. When we got there I saw Terri.

"How did this happen!" I screamed.

"I was only gone for a couple of minutes I didn't think that John would find us!" Terri cried.

While talking to Terri the doctors came in.

"We're looking for the family of Kiera Ross and Starmeka Miller."

We all jumped up at the same time.

"Is everyone here family?"

"Yes," we all said.

"Okay well we were able to stop Kiera Ross from bleeding so she's stable but Starmeka Miller didn't make it."

I didn't hear anything after that. It was as if I went deaf, I got light headed, and my knees went weak and I began falling but Julez caught me.

"Royal, Royal are you alright?" Terri asked.

"Don't touch me!"

"Royal?"

"This is all your fault!"

"I'm sorry!"

"This is all your fault!" I cried, screaming, trying to get my hands on her.

"Come on baby let's take you home," Juelz said.

"No, no, no!" I cried.

"Come on baby," Juelz said.

"It's your fault, I hate you, I fucking hate you!" I screamed at Terri.

"I'm sorry," she cried.

Juelz picked me up and took me outside of the hospital. When we made it outside he put me inside of his truck and we drove off. I cried the whole ride home until I couldn't cry anymore.

"Do you want me to come inside with you?" he asked.

"No my mom is home."

"Are you going to be alright?"

"Yea."

"Well call me if you need me."

"Okay."

He leaned over and gave me a very tight hug and then he hopped out the truck, came and opened my door for me, and he walked me to the front door.

"If you want to talk call me."

"Okay."

He hugged me once more and went and got inside the truck. I entered the house and to my surprise my mom was waiting for me.

"So you still decided to date this boy after I forbid it?"

"Not right now ma, this is not a good time."

"Oh this is a great time; you think you grown and that you can go against my wishes, well I've already packed your bags you need to leave."

"You know I always knew for you to be bull headed but I never thought of you as being careless but I'll just add that on too."

"I don't care what you add on but I hope that, that boy is worth all your troubles."

"You know you so worried about Juelz that you didn't even care to ask your daughter, with swollen, red, eyes what's wrong with her but since you're insensitive I'll tell you anyway my friends were robbed, raped, and stabbed tonight and one passed away!"

"Oh sweetie I'm so sorry."

"No I don't want your sympathy now."

I pulled out my phone and I called Juelz.

"Hello."

"Turn around I'm moving with you."

"I'll be there in a couple of minutes."

"Okay."

I got off the phone with Juelz and I started taking my bags outside.

"Sweetie you don't have to leave, I'm sorry!"

"I have heard that line enough for tonight and honestly I'm sick of hearing it!"

"Well at least let me fix you a cup of tea."

"You really don't want me to tell you what you can do with that tea."

"Well I've already apologized for it what more do you want me to do."

"For once I want you to try stepping off your high horse because you too high up that you're lost and I don't want to be a part of this roller coaster anymore!" I walked out the door and Juelz was just pulling up. He got out the truck and he put my bags in the trunk. I went upstairs, grabbed my stash, and I put it in my purse. I went down stairs and gave my mom a hug and a kiss.

"I love you."

And I walked out of the door. Thirty minutes later we made it to Juelz house. He took my bags inside and he helped me unpack silently. After everything had been put up I laid in the bed and Juelz lay behind me.

"Juelz I have something to tell you?"

"Can it wait you're grieving right now."

"No, this can't wait, look I know that we promised to never keep a secret from each other but I didn't tell you everything."

"Okay."

"The day that you dropped me off at Kiera house Terri let us know about these drugs and guns that she had stolen from a man name John, she talked about selling them and then she said that it would be a onetime deal. At first I was against it but then I seen that everyone else was in and I didn't want to be the only one left out so I agree to it. But after they had gotten robbed I backed out but Terri went and got some more because she had gotten use to the fast money."

"You did what?"

"I'm sorry I know that I should have went with my first instinct but at the time what she was saying made so much since."

"I can't believe you, how can you even think about stepping into something so dangerous?"

"I don't know!" I cried.

"So ya'll know who killed your friend?"

"Yes."

"Well why you didn't tell her mother?"

"Because she will hate me forever."

"But it was Terri's idea!"

"But we should have said no, I knew it was a bad idea we should have just said no!" I cried.

"It's going to be okay."

If I thought that night was bad the rest of the days was even worst, I couldn't eat and I couldn't sleep because every time I closed my eyes I thought about what I should have said or what I should have done. I had gone to see Kiera but she had gone from being stable to going into Acoma. I felt so responsible and angry, I was responsible for not talking them out of it and angry at Terri for even bringing it into our lives. I hadn't seen Terri in a while but word on the street was that John was still looking for her. That day I received an invitation for Star's funeral in the mail and that's when it really started hitting home. My best friend that I had grew up with and called whenever I needed to talk was gone forever and it was my entire fault. I couldn't bear it so I looked in the medicine cabinet and I took a bottle of aspirin. I went into a deep sleep and I had a dream about Star. She was smiling and walking towards me. She came up to me and she put her hand on my face.

"You're not supposed to be here."

"I can't live knowing that I'm the cause of this."

"This is not your fault. You couldn't have done anything to change this and I don't want you living your life like this."

"But I'm not living my soul died when you left."

"Your soul is not dead, and you can't go around feeling sorry for yourself. My family, Kiera's family, Kiera, and Terri needs you right now you're their strength so you take all those negative feelings and turn them into something positive. But god haven't sent for you so you have to go back, but before you leave make me one promise."

"And what's that?"

"Promise me that you will find Terri and forgive her."

"How am I supposed to forgive her?"

"Find it in your heart" she said as she hugged, kissed me on the cheek, and disappeared into the light. When I opened my eyes I was in the hospital and my mom and Juelz was by my side. I couldn't stop the tears from falling I just began crying.

"Baby is you okay?" Juelz asked.

"Sweetie." mom cried.

"I'm fine."

"What was you thinking about?" Juelz asked.

"I just wanted to be free."

"So you were just going to forget about all the people that loves you?" he asked.

"I'm sorry," I said.

"Honey are you feeling okay?" My mom asked.

"Yea I'm feeling fine.

They sat with me all night until it was time for all of my visitors to leave. The next morning it was time for me to be discharged but they wanted to make sure that I wasn't suicidal so they released me in the care of my mother. I stayed with my mom for a couple of days then I returned back home.

"Baby do you want something to eat?" Juelz asked.

"No thank you."

"What you doing?"

"Trying to find me something to wear to the funeral."

"Are you sure that you're strong enough to go?"

"Yes I'm fine."

"I'm just making sure."

"I'm not going to try and kill myself again if that's what you mean."

"Ms. Royal that's not what I meant it's just that I don't want you blaming yourself again"

"I'm not baby I'm fine"

"Okay."

"Are you going?"

"Of course I got to go to support you."

I got in the shower, got dressed, put my hair in a ponytail, and we left to go to the funeral. When we first got there I was scared but as Star would say I finally got the courage to face my fears. When I looked around there was so many people and half of the people I didn't even know. I didn't even realize that Star had such a great impact on so many people lives. I went and found me somewhere to sit while the pastor preached. After the pastor was done he asked if there was someone that would like to say something. I looked around for a minute but no one came so I stood up and I walked to the stage.

"I will like to come and say my last goodbyes. You know Star and I met in pre k and she was one of the best friends that anyone could ever ask for. I can't count how many times I had problems and I was able to call her and she would give me great advice and even if she couldn't do anything about it she was willing to come over so that she could put a smile on my face. Just last month my birthday came around and we took a trip to California and if I would have known that, that would be the last time that I really got to spend time with her I would have made the best out of it but I was so busy moping around that I couldn't really enjoy myself but if I could go back in time there's definitely some things that I would change. They say that you never know when it's someone last days, so cherish every moment so people listen to the saying because I missed my moment."

I went outside to get myself together and to gather my thoughts.

"Are you okay?" Juelz asked.

"Yea I'm fine I just needed some air."

"Do you need anything to drink?"

"No thank you."

While talking Star aunt came out side.

"I'm going to excuse ya'll for a minute," Juelz said.

When he got up and left she came and sat right next to me.

"So how are you holding up?" She asked.

"I'm okay but I should be asking you that question?"

"I'm taking it day by day."

"Mrs. Walker there's something I have to tell you."

"What is it?"

"Some months' back Terri came telling us about some drugs and guns that she had stolen from her boyfriend and she wanted to sell them. At first we all was against it but then she managed to convince all of us that we would do this once and get out but after everything was gone she went and got more because she liked the fast money. I backed out because I felt that it was dangerous but they continued. I'm so sorry I should have tried to talk her out of it!" I cried.

"It's not your fault."

"Yes, it is, she was my best friend, and I should have tried to stop her."

"You girls are young and you guys are going to make all kinds of mistakes in your life and Star just was at the wrong place at the wrong time. You could have tried to talk her out of it until you turned blue in the face but once Star made up her mind she wasn't going to change it trust me I know. So just wipe those tears away because Star wouldn't want to see you like that."

She gave me a hug and we went back inside and I caught up with Juelz. I went around talking to some of Star's family and friends and just talking to them made me think that she was in the room. I stayed around for another hour hoping to see Terri but she was a no show. I went home that night and I felt different, I felt free because I had got everything off of my chest. I went upstairs and I went and took me a hot bubble bath, got dress, and went to bed. The next morning, I woke up to breakfast in bed.

"What's the occasion?" I asked.

"Nothing I just wanted to show you that I care, but there is something that I have to talk to you about."

"Okay."

"I got to go out of town to make a drop so I want to know will you be okay here by yourself."

"I'm going to be fine but you better make that drop and come right back home."

"Yes mam but you better be here when I get back."

"As long as you continue to be a good boy I'll always be here when you get back."

"Bet."

He gave me a hug and a kiss, packed his bag, and left but not before I reminded him what he would be missing if he messed up. Afterwards I went to the door and watched him drive off. The next morning while preparing breakfast I received a call.

"Hello."

"Hi this is Dr. Anderson from Georgia town hospital."

"Oh my god is something wrong?"

"Is this Royal Wilkinson?"

"Yes what's the problem?"

"There's no problem, I was calling because Kiera Ross has woken up from being in a coma and the first person that she asked for was you."

"Oh my god I'm on my way!"

I turned off the stove, ran and got in my car, and rushed to the hospital. When I got there I almost forgot to check in.

"Excuse me ms but you have to check in first," the nurse said.

"Oh I'm so sorry."

I went back and checked in and I ran to Kiera's room. When I made it inside Kiera was already sitting up like nothing ever happened. I didn't wait for her to say anything I just ran over and hugged her as tight as I could and we stayed like that for a minute just crying. After we both had calmed down.

"I thought I was dead."

"I prayed for you everyday."

And then before I could say anything else she asked me the biggest question that I dreaded answering.

"So where is Star and Terri?"

"Sweetie I don't think that we should talk about this right now."

"Talk about what?"

"So do you want anything to eat or drink?"

"Royal where is Star and Terri stop being around the bush?"

"I don't know where Terri is but Star didn't make it."

"It's ok I'll just call and talk to her."

"No Kiera, Star didn't make it, she passed away."

"No, no, no, noooo!" she said crying.

We hugged, I cried with her, and then it was as if I was reliving it all over again. I closed my eyes and I wished that it was all just a dream but when I opened my eyes back and I still held Kiera in my arms I knew that it wasn't.

"We should have listen to you, we made a big mistake," Kiera said.

"Come on Kiera calm down please!"

"I'm so sorry, she wanted to quit when you did but I ask her to do one more week, I'm so sorry!"

"Kiera stop it, it's nobody's fault we all made a dumb decision."

"That should have been me; I should have been the one that died."

"Stop talking like that!"

"No when they came in to rob us Star was in the back so they didn't even know that she was there, she came out with a knife to try and fight them off and he beat her, raped her, and stabbed her while John held me and made me watch, I closed my eyes so I couldn't see while struggling and trying to break free of his hold but, when I didn't hear her screaming anymore I opened my eyes and she just lay there in a pool of blood. I should have been the one that was killed, why did she have to try and save me, why."

"It's not your fault and you can't keep blaming yourself and who is he."

"I don't really remember his face but I definitely remember his voice."

"Did he wear a mask?"

"No it's just that after Star went silent I went blank; I didn't feel anything that was done to me I was too numb."

"I wished that this was a dream so many times."

"Me too, so what happened with Terri?"

"Well when I found out about you and Star I blamed her and after that I didn't see her again, she didn't show up at the funeral, she didn't come to the hospital, and her phone has been disconnected."

"Do you think that she's okay?"

"I don't know, I wanted to apologize but it's as if she disappeared off the face of the earth, you know my mind was so messed up that I went from blaming her to blaming myself, I even tried to take my own life."

"It's really nobody's fault, we all knew what we were doing and the kind of danger that we were facing, I guess when you're young you make stupid decision but I'll give anything to go back in time and change it all."

"You and me both."

Chapter 10

We talked for a while until she went to sleep and then I left to go home. While I was driving it hit me. It was so crazy how it took something like this for either one of us to open our eyes. I mean there's a lot of people that make mistakes but most times they get a second chance at life, I guess Star wasn't so lucky because her first mistake was her last, it never dawned on me that at the time Terri and I should have been consoling each other but I needed someone to blame besides myself. I mean who's to say if I would have stuck to no that Star and Kiera wouldn't have change their minds. Well now I would never know because what was done was done and Star was gone. I finally pulled up in front of the house and I went inside to do nothing but sit and think. While thinking I realized that the whole time I had been looking for Terri I hadn't thought to stop by her parent's house to check and see had they seen her. So just as fast as I had sat down I got up to go over to her parent's place. It took me about an hour to get there, when I finally made it in front of the house I took a breather before I rang the doorbell. I expected for her to curse me out or something when she opened the door but instead she greeted me with opened arms.

"Oh sweetie how have you been?"

"Fine and you?" I asked returning the hug.

"I've been okay, come on in don't just stand there."

I entered the house and I found me a seat in the living room.

"Would you like anything to drink?"

"No thank you I'm fine."

She came and found her a seat right next to mines.

"Well you look a little worried is there anything that I can do for you."

"Yes mam as a matter of fact you can, I was wondering by any chance had Terri stopped by here."

"Well I would love to help you with that but the truth of the matter is I haven't seen Terri in two weeks."

"Do you have any idea where she may have gone?"

"No, all of our family stays out of town, why what's going on."

"Nothing I just really wanted to find Terri and apologize for what I said to her and I also wanted her to know that Kiera has awaken and that she's looking for her."

"I'm so happy, you girls have been friends since you were all little girls and you girls was the only friends that she ever had and knew, look there's a lot of things that I could say but the fact of the matter is none of those things would bring Star back."

"Look Mrs. Davison, at the time I guess I just needed someone to blame and I'm sorry for that because we all had our own brain and we all had a part in it but at the end of the day we're all sisters and instead of me being angry with her I should have been holding her and letting her know that everything would be alright."

"You know everyone makes mistakes but it takes a real woman to admit when she's wrong and sweetie you have developed into a very beautiful woman."

"Thank you Mrs. Davison, but if you see Terri please let her know that I stopped by," I said hugging her.

"I most definitely will."

I got up and I left and went straight home. I felt so relieved like a lot of stress had been lifted off of my shoulders. I went upstairs, took a hot bubble bath, and then I took a nap. This time as I dreamed about star she didn't say anything she just smiled. Two months had passed since that had happened and Kiera was now at home and visiting on a regular basic, I still hadn't heard from Terri but I still kept my eyes and ears opened.

"Good morning Ms. Royal."

"Good morning Juelz."

"So the last couple of months have been interesting so what do you say that we go out tonight and dance off a lot of steam."

"That's fine and all but where would we go?"

"My home boy Trent throwing a party tonight at the club for this new artist that he producing and he invited me and my lady."

"That's nice, can I invite Kiera?"

"Yea that's your girl she can come along."

"What time are we leaving?"

"Nine o'clock."

"Okay I'll be ready but other than that what do you have planned for today."

"Nothing I might just stop by my sister house to see her and the triplets."

"Not without me mister I want to see them too."

"Good because they have been asking about you and my mom supposed to be coming up here in a couple of days."

"Good now when she comes in town I can prepare her a real meal."

"Oh really and what kind of meal are you going to prepare for me?"

"I'm not going to prepare any meal for you right now because I have to meet up with Kiera at the mall in Twenty minutes."

"Come on baby how am I supposed to get my day started without my most important meal."

"And what meal is that?"

"Breakfast."

"Well, breakfast is on the stove."

"You know what I'm talking about, come on just let me get a quickie."

"Your quickies turn into hours!"

"I promise I'll be quick."

"Okay but you know this determines if you ever get a quickie ever again."

"Yes mam," he said as he carried me upstairs. After giving Juelz a full course meal I quickly took a shower and hurried off to meet up with Kiera. When I got there she was sitting inside the food court.

"So what took you so long miss busy body?"

"I'm sorry something came up."

"Something or someone."

"Oh don't you start with me missy because I heard about your new man."

"Okay who told you?"

"Juelz and his friend that you are dating."

"I'm going to kill both of them."

"Well I can't allow you to kill Juelz because I will be lonely and miserable and I know you not going to kill Siy because you would miss him."

"Yea you might be right, but anyway let's get to the shopping."

"Oh don't forget to find something for tonight."

"Why, what's going on tonight?"

"Siy didn't tell you that one of their homeboys is having a party tonight."

"He said something about it but I was kind of occupied at the time."

"Yea so what are you wearing?"

"I don't know I might wear something simple like a pair of denim shorts with a fitted top, so what about you?"

"I don't know I might wear a dress."

"Come on girl it's a party where you dance and get loose, I mean I like dresses too but you can't really enjoy yourself in a dress."

"Yea you right, okay what about some blue jean pants with some kind of top."

"That's sounds great with the exception of some kind of top."

"I know but I'll figure out what kind while we shop."

"Okay let's go."

We walked through the mall shopping. We went into like six or seven stores but with all this stuff it was so worth it. After shopping so much we finally had a chance to relax so we went into the food court and found us something to eat. It felt so good to be shopping with one of my best friends I mean this wasn't the first time that we had done this but after what had, had happened a couple of months ago I definitely didn't want it to be my last. I had lost one friend, another was missing, and Kiera was here in my face and I didn't know who would leave the world first and I didn't want to miss out on spending anytime with one of my best friends.

"Ro-Ro did you hear me?"

"I'm sorry what did you say."

"I said thank you for getting me out of the house."

"Girl please what are best friends for."

"Ro-Ro are you okay?"

"Yea I'm fine sometimes I just stare off into space."

"Well there's a reason that you staring off into space so what's wrong."

"I was just thinking about all the things that happened."

"Come on girl we supposed to be having fun, so no sad thoughts, okay."

"Okay."

We talked some more, finished eating, and then we left. When I made it home Juelz was just getting out of the shower.

"So are you ready to go/"

"Can I just rest my feet because they are tired from all the walking that we did?"

"I see why," he said looking at all the bags.

"Well hey I'm a woman and we have a lot of choices we can't just choose one or two things."

"Baby you are a shopaholic."

"I am not."

"Prove it."

"How?"

"No shopping for a week."

"Okay that hurts but I'm willing to take you up on your challenge so what do I get if I win."

"Anything you want and I get anything I want if you lose bet."

"Bet!"

I watched Juelz get dressed while I tried my best to rest. After he was done we left to go and visit his sister. When we made it there Portia greeted us and invited us in. when we made it inside we noticed that the girls were nowhere to be found.

"So where are the girls?" Juelz asked.

"Their dad came and pick them up for the weekend."

"Portia I told you we were coming."

"I know but he just popped up I didn't know he was coming, don't be mad they'll be back Sunday."

"Yea right."

"So Portia what have you been up to?" I asked breaking the ice.

"Nothing much, but I have started dating again."

"That's great so who is this special guy and when do we get to meet him."

"Well his name is Chase and we have been dating for one and a half months and you will actually get to meet him tomorrow when we stop by ya'll house."

"Yea well he better, have his mind right," Juelz said.

"Why you always got to be so nasty when I start dating."

"Because if someone is going to date my sister they better be on they grown man-ish."

"Coming from the man who thinks that dealing drugs in the street is a job."

"Yea, you heard what I said."

"Okay this is not about me dating so what's the real deal."

"I know that man didn't just pop up out of the blue and decide that he wanted to be a father so what did you do."

"Okay so I saw him in the store with his wife and I reminded him that he had kids and I threaten him with child support."

"And you're comfortable with sending them with a man that was forced to acknowledge his own kids."

"Juelz I don't want my kids to grow up without a father I mean we did and look how...."

She stopped herself.

"Naw don't stop, go ahead and say it, look I how I turned out, yea well my dad wasn't around because he was killed it wasn't because he chose not to be."

"I didn't mean it like that Juelz."

"Naw you said it just like you meant to, come on Royal let's go."

"But Juelz!" I pleaded.

"Royal let's go."

"I'm so sorry," I told Portia as I grabbed my purse and left.

We rode in silence the whole way home. When we finally made it home he went into the theater room and I went upstairs. I couldn't believe what had just happened I was so frustrated that I dozed off for a minute. When I woke up Juelz was standing over me.

"Are you going to get ready for the party?" he asked.

"No I'm not going."

"What do you mean you're not going?"

"Just what I said."

"What's wrong with you?"

"What's wrong with me, I'm so tired of being shut out of your life when you get upset and then you feel that everything is supposed to be okay when you're ready to talk."

"Royal can we talk about this later we got a party to attend to."

"You go right ahead and attend the party you don't need me it's like I don't exist anyway."

"Okay, what do you want me to do?"

"Nothing, if you don't know then I don't know," I got up out of the bed.

"Where you going?"

"I'm getting ready for the party, ain't that what you want."

"Do you want to talk about it?"

"No I'm good."

I got into the shower and got ready for the party. While in the car once again we rode in silence. When we made it inside the club I walked away from Juelz and I went to find Kiera. Five minutes into the search I found her sitting at the table with Siy.

"Hey girl," she said hugging me.

"Hey"

"Where my boy at?" Siy asked.

"I don't know he somewhere in the crowd."

"When ya'll women do that, that can't be a good sign so I'm going to excuse myself, let ya'll talk, and go find my boy."

He got up and left.

"Okay so what happened?" Kiera asked.

"Girl what didn't happen, we went to see his sister he basically cussed her out, yelled at me, and then decided not to talk to me until he felt like it."

"Men."

"Tell me about it, but I came to enjoy myself so I'm blocking him out."

The whole night my girl and I talked, laughed, danced, and enjoyed ourselves. After we were tired of dancing we went to sit back at our table when this tall, brown skin, brotha came and approached our table.

"I figured that you ladies could use a drink after dancing for so long."

"Thank you," we both said.

He pulled up a seat and sat next to me.

"So what's your name pretty lady?"

"My name is Royal."

"Well Royal my name is Cody."

"Nice to meet you Cody."

"Nice to meet you too, so Royal do you have a man?"

"Yes I do have a man I'm actually here with him tonight."

"Well I haven't seen you with anybody all night."

"So you didn't see a man trying to offer me food or something to drink."

"I mean I seen that but he just looked like a guy trying to hit on you."

"No that's my boyfriend."

"Well what boyfriend don't know won't hurt him."

"Well that's about to change because he's heading this way," Kiera said.

"If you don't mind can you leave because this could get ugly?"

"No I'll protect you."

"I don't need protection but you on the other hand might do."

"I'm not worried."

"Hi Juelz," Kiera greeted him trying to keep him away from the table.

"What's up?" he said walking around her.

As he got closer I started sweating because this couldn't be good. So I stood up and wrapped my arms around him.

"Hey baby you want to dance?" I asked.

"Yea in a minute, so what ya'll doing?"

"Nothing Cody just offered Kiera and I a drink and he was just leaving."

"Well actually I was trying to see was this beautiful young lady spoken for."

"Well now you know."

"Yea maybe another time Royal, I left my number on a napkin why don't you give me a call sometimes."

"You must didn't hear me the first time."

"Oh I heard you loud and clear."

"Let me explain something to you man this ain't what you want just walk away."

"Is that a threat?"

"See I don't make threats because I always follow up on my word."

"Baby lets go," I said pulling on his arm.

"I'm sorry but are you trying to intimidate me?"

"(Laughing) Ah man who is this clown?" Juelz said.

Trent heard the commotion and he came to see what was going on.

"Is everything good Juelz?" Trent asked.

"I'm good it's him that you need to be worried about."

"He don't need to worry about me I can hold my own," Cody said.

"You got thirty seconds not minutes to get the fuck up out my face."

"Or what?"

Juelz smiled for a minute and then he pulled out his gun and pointed it at Cody's face. Cody looked scared with his hands in the air.

"Let's go Juelz," I said.

I looked in Juelz eyes and the Juelz that I knew was gone.

"Baby please let's just go he didn't mean anything by it," I said kissing on him. He looked at me and he lowered his gun and Cody took off running as if he was in a track meet. We made it to the dance floor and Juelz wrapped his arms around my waist.

"So you were going to replace me with that clown?"

"If I was going to replace you I wouldn't be standing here with you right now."

"You really think that I'll let you go like that?"

"I don't know maybe."

"Please you stuck with me forever."

"Oh is that right?"

"That's right."

Chapter 11

We danced all night until we got so tired that we just couldn't dance anymore and then we returned home, made love and fell to sleep in each other's arm. The next morning, we woke up to a knock at the door. I followed Juelz down the stairs and when the door swung open it was Juelz mother.

"Hey ma I didn't know that you were coming this early."

"I wasn't but I said that if I can make it hours earlier then that would leave me with more time to do what I planned."

"And what exactly is that."

"That's for me to know and for you to find out."

While they were talking I ran upstairs and went to jump in the shower. When I was done I got dressed and returned back downstairs.

"Well don't you move fast missy I turned my head for one minute and you were gone."

"I know and I'm sorry I didn't mean to be rude but I just had to get into some appropriate attire."

"Child please I know the life of being young, in love, and living all alone and that my dear is such a beautiful experience."

"Ma really," Juelz said.

"Boy hush how do you think that you got here you better stop feeling like you're the only one that has ever been young."

"I know that you were young before too but I don't want to hear about those times."

"Well maybe if you listen to some of my times you might just learn a few things believe me you I still got a lot of things that I could teach you two."

"Ma its 2014 everything has upgraded since then including that."

"That's what I'm trying to tell you."

"I know that's right," I replied.

"Don't influence her" Juelz said.

"She's not influencing anything she just letting you know"

"Well can we talk about something else?"

"Of course so what is it that you would like to talk about?"

"How was your flight?"

"It was okay with the exception of a crying baby that was basically screaming for attention but his mother couldn't see that because she was so busy playing with her computer."

"Very interesting."

"Yea I guess, so Royal do you have plans today?" she asked.

"No not today."

"Well that's just great because I have a great day planned out for us."

"Okay so should I go change my clothes?"

"No you look fine."

"Okay."

While in the middle of our conversation someone rang the doorbell.

"I got it," I said.

I answered the door and it was Portia.

"Hi I hope I'm not intruding," she said.

"No Portia you know that you're always welcomed here come in."

"Are you sure that my brother will be okay with that?"

"I don't care if your brother will be okay with it or not I said it's fine now get your butt in here."

Portia came inside and I showed her to the living room where we all were sitting,

"Hey everybody, look who showed up!"

"What are you doing here Portia?" Juelz asked.

"I came to Discuss what happen last night."

"We ain't got nothing to discuss you said everything that you had to say last night."

"Look maybe this was a bad idea."

"Yea it was now get out."

"Don't you move a muscle!," I said.

"What?" Juelz asked.

"You heard what I said."

"So after what was said last night you expect me to let her sit in my house, (Laughing) you must be joking, now I said get out!" he yelled.

"And I said stay, now Portia is not perfect but neither are you, you make mistakes too so you either fix this are she won't be the only one walking out the door," I said.

"Look I came to apologize about what I said, look I know that you care about the girls as if they were your own but I want my kids to have both of their parents in their lives and if I have to act a little crazy for that to happen then I have no problem with doing that."

"I understand that but forcing him to do his part won't make him a great father you don't know how he treating them let alone his wife, why don't you wait for him to come around or wait until their old enough to make their own decisions."

"Because by then it will be too late."

"Well that will fall back on him but for now you just be the best mother that you can possibly be."

"Yea I guess that, that make sense."

"Now that's more like it," I said.

"Yes, it is, now that we got that out of the way I have someone that I will like for ya'll to meet," Portia said.

"Where they at?" Juelz asked.

Portia went outside and came back in with a man about six feet tall, high yellow, nice build, a beautiful smile, and a fade.

"Everyone this is my boyfriend Chase."

"Nice to meet you Chase," we all said.

"It's nice to meet you all too."

"So what do you do?" Juelz asked.

"I'm an English teacher at a middle school."

"And how long have you been doing that."

"For about seven years now."

"Do you like children?"

"I love children and that's what helped me to choose my career."

"Do you have any children of your own?"

"No."

"Do you want any?"

"Yes of course."

"How do you feel about my sister having three kids"

"I'm excited to get to know them and to build a family with them, look I grew up with a step father in my life because my father didn't want to step up to the plate and take care of his responsibility so I was thankful for my step father because everyone deserves a father figure in their lives I mean honestly did any of us ask to be here, so why should we have to pay the price of something that our parents did or did not do."

"That was a very smart answer; I think I'm going to like you."

"Now that the twenty-five questions are over with just make yourself comfortable, now would you like something to drink?" I asked.

"Sure how about a beer?"

"Coming right up."

I went into the kitchen and I got two beers one for Juelz and one for Chase. I returned back to the living room and I handed them their beers.

"Okay everyone I'm enjoying this family reunion and all but I'm going to have to steal your women for a couple of hours," Juelz mom said.

"Hold on now, Ms. Royal can't leave this house until I say so."

"Juelz you better sit your butt down because you don't run nothing but your mouth, I brought you into this world and I'll take you out!"

"(Laughing) I know that's right Marie," I said.

"You might have won this one but what are you going to do when she goes back home."

"All she got to do is call and I'll be there."

We hugged and kissed our men and we headed out of the door. We drove for a while before we arrived at the mall.

"Ok ladies now it's time for us to shop until we drop," Juelz mom said.

"You ain't got to tell me more than once because I'm much in need of some sexy clothing," Portia said.

We went into each clothing store shopping until we could shop no more. After we were done with that we went into the food court, ordered us some food, and began talking.

"So Portia, Chase seems to be a nice guy," I said.

"He is but I'm kind of worried about what the girls might think, I mean they pretty much get alone with everyone but they've never met him so I just don't know."

"Well maybe you should sit them down and talk to them before you introduce them," I said.

"I'm glad that you girls are getting along and everything but I have something that I want to tell you."

"What's that"? Portia and I both asked.

"I'm getting married."

"Oh my god congratulations," I said.

"Yea congratulations mama but have you told Juelz yet."

"Not yet but Juelz is a grown man so he will understand."

"I know he's grown mama but you know how he felt about daddy."

"Yea, if you like I could tell him instead," I said.

"No thank you, I think that I can do it Juelz is just going to have to get over it."

We talked for a while about our love lives before we returned home. When we made it inside the men were in front of the television watching sports. Everyone sat a little while longer before they left to go home. And when they were gone I began cleaning.

"So how was your day with ma dukes"

"Oh it was great."

"I see you brought at least six bags in the house."

"Oh and trust when I say you're going to love every piece inside of them."

"Well in that case I can't wait to see what you got for me tonight because you lost that bet."

"Yea I know so were, you surprised with Chase."

"Yea I was because I thought that I would have to put someone in the head lock."

"You thought you would or you were hoping you could."

"A little bit of both."

He started to kiss on my neck.

"Uh, uh, uh, tonight I'm in control."

"Oh really?"

"Yea really, so go upstairs and when I'm done here I'll come up."

"Don't keep me waiting."

"I won't."

He headed upstairs and I finished cleaning the house. When I was done I went upstairs to take a shower. After getting out I dried my body, shaved, lotion my body, put on my expensive perfume and then I put on my red, knitted, lingerie dress, with my red thong underneath. I straighten my hair and put on my makeup and when I was sure that everything was exactly how I wanted it I exit the bathroom.

"Well, well, well, Ms. Royal it seems as if you're trying to give me a heart attack."

"Who little old me."

"Yea now bring your fine self over here."

"Come and get me daddy."

He came over to me, picked me up, and pinned me against the wall. He began biting and sucking on my neck. I dug my nails into his back while I gripped my legs around his waist.

"I want you inside of me right now," I whispered.

"Be patient baby," he whispered back.

He laid me down softly on the bed, slowly undressed me, and began sucking on my breast. I moaned really loud as I arched my back to the vibration that came through my body.

"Baby please I can't take this anymore!"

He said nothing as he kissed and licked my stomach until he made it to my wetness. I gripped the sheets really tight, moaning very loudly until my body began to shake as if I was going into shock. Finally, he slowly entered my body, I dug my nails into his back while we kissed, slowly making love, trying every position that we could think of, until both of our bodies shook and we fell asleep in each other's arms. A couple of weeks had gone by and things between Juelz and I had started to change I mean everything between us was an argument. I was just so frustrated and I needed a break so I called my girl Kiera and we decided to meet up at the mall. I took a shower, got dressed, and I left without even telling him or without even saying goodbye. When I made it inside the mall we walked around the store window shopping finally after a while we made it to the food court, had a seat, and we began talking.

"So Royal what's going on?"

"Girl Juelz is getting on my last nerve I mean with us just being in the same room agitates me."

"What is he doing?"

"Breathing."

"You don't mean that."

"Yes I do I just need a break."

"I know what you need, you need one of those big burgers and fries from King's Beef."

"Girl I don't want they mess all of it is starting to taste like dog food to me."

"No girl because that's your favorite restaurant."

"Girl I'm for real they food taste different and not in a good way."

"Ohhhhhh I know what you need."

"What?"

"Come on follow me."

I hoped in my car and I followed her to the nearest pharmacy. When we made it inside she went all the way to the back and home girl had the audacity to pick up a pregnancy test.

"Girl are you crazy I'm not taking that mess because I'm not pregnant."

"Well if you not then you don't have anything to worry about so you can take the test with no problem."

"Okay so what do I get when it comes out negative?"

"I'll take you on a well needed trip but if it comes out positive then you have to pay for a trip for the both of us."

"Ok that's a bet but I'm going to have to take over your house because I don't want Juelz to think anything."

"Ok."

Kiera bought the test, we hoped in our cars, and I followed her back to her house. I let her go inside first to look around for Siy.

"Ok girl the coast is clear".

I went inside the house and I went straight to the bathroom to take the test. After thirty minutes of waiting I went and read it and my worst nightmare was staring at me in big bold letters it read Positive.

"Well what does it say?"

"It says abortion."

"Girl Juelz will kill you and you can't pay for a trip if you are dead."

"That's why we not going to tell him."

"Come on Royal why you tripping you know you would love to have a baby by Juelz."

"A month or two ago that would have been nice but now I really don't know so until I figure out what to do I'm not going to tell him."

"Now Royal how long do you think you can hide a pregnancy from him"

"As long as I want."

While in the middle of our conversation Siy pulled up.

"Girl Siy just pulled up."

"Ok just give me the bag, the box, and the receipt."

I got everything from Kiera and I stuffed everything in my purse and when he walked in we acted like everything was normal.

"What's up Royal?"

"Hey Siy what's going on?"

"Nothing much what ya'll doing?"

"Nothing we was just sitting around talking but I'll just call you later Kiera."

"Alright."

I got in my car, found the biggest dumpster and I threw all the evidence away. When I made it home Juelz was upstairs sleeping so I decided to take me a nap on the sofa. I slept for almost three hours before I woke up and realized that someone was standing over me.

"Why are you just standing staring at me like a zombie?"

"So this how we going to be?"

"How?"

"Sleeping in a different part of the house like we not even together?"

"I didn't want to disturb you."

"You full of shit so where were you!"

"I was with my friend."

"What friend?"

"My friend Kiera and what's with all the questions?"

"So when did you start leaving the house without even saying a word to me?"

"When everything is said to you became an argument."

"You make everything out of in argument I just choose to walk away from it."

"Well walk away from this."

In the middle of our conversation we got a knock at the door and when he opened it my heart dropped because I thought that I was busted.

"What's up Siy?"

"Bro we got some business to handle!"

"A'ight I'll be out there in a minute."

He turned his attention back to me.

"So what are you about to do?"

"What do you mean what am I about to do what you expect me to do in the house, look you don't care anyway just go on and run the street with your friends."

"I got some business to handle I'll be back."

"Like I said do what you do!"

He tried to kiss me but I turned my head away and I watched as he walked out the door. I went upstairs and I ran me a bubble bath, lit me some candles, and I lied back in the tub to relax.

"Hello little person inside me, look I don't know the first thing about being a parent so if this conversation becomes weird just tune me out, listen I'm really not a strong believer when it comes to abortions but sometimes you have to figure out what's best for you, yea I know I should have thought about that before I went down this path but I thought that things would be different. At first your daddy was someone that I would have had a million babies with, that is when we would have gotten married but something in him has changed and I do not like it and besides I'm sure that god could have chosen a much better mother than me. Anyway my decision isn't clear yet so don't get too antsy."

Chapter 12

I finished taking my bath, got dressed, and I called it a night. Another week had passed and Juelz's birthday was in a couple of days, we had started to get along a little better but I still hadn't told him the news. I had been shopping with his mother and sister for his surprise birthday party whenever they came and visit, but I told Juelz that I had nothing planned. Everything was going as planned but in order for me to keep his mind off of his birthday I had to keep him busy so today I was taking him to his sister house because she was having a dinner.

"Come on bae we going to be late."

"Well she can wait she know her big brother got to get fresh."

"I hope you explain all of that to her when we make it there."

"I will."

After he was finally done getting ready we hopped in the car and headed to Portia's house. We managed to make it on time and she stood at the door greeting everyone.

"Hey ya'll I'm glad that ya'll could make it."

"Yea well, messing with your brother we almost didn't."

"You don't have to tell me I know that he is a pretty boy."

"I just had to let you know that it wouldn't have been my fault."

"Girl I know he's been like that since we were little."

When we made it inside everyone greeted and got to know one another. People watched sports, played cards, barbequed outside, and some even just sat around talking. While walking around the house I bumped into Juelz mother.

"Hi Royal," she said hugging me.

"Hi Marie."

"Did you get to meet everyone?"

"Almost."

"Well don't worry you have all night to do that."

"I hope so because so far everyone is so nice and laid back."

"Yea that's how our family is, but let me ask you a question."

"Okay go ahead."

"Do you have something that you want to tell me?"

"No why do you ask?"

"Because your curves are becoming a little wider."

"Marie what are you trying to say?"

"Are you pregnant?"

"No."

"Well you could have fooled me but I'm going to be watching you ms thang because either you're not telling me or you don't even know yet."

My heart began beating fast because although I didn't want Juelz to know because I was unsure of what to do I didn't want to lie to his mother either because she was so nice.

"Ok wait please don't tell anyone else!"

"So I was right I'm about to be a grandma," she whispered

"Yes but please don't tell anyone else not even Juelz."

"Ok so that means that I'm the first one to know."

"The second my friend knew first."

"Oh congratulations baby," she said hugging me. "And don't worry your secret is safe with me."

"Thank you."

The rest of night went on smoothly. We had so much fun and when we finally made it home I managed to do nothing but go to sleep. Two days later it was Juelz twenty second birthday and I had to get him out of the house if Kiera and I planned on putting up any decorations so I called Siy over.

"Bae hurry up Siy is waiting for you."

"Man that nigga can wait it's a real boss birthday."

"Well, boss you gon be walking to the gym soon because I'm ready to shoot some hoops."

"A'ight man I'm coming."

Five minutes later Juelz came walking down stairs with his basketball attire on.

"Alright Ms. Royal I'll see you when I get back," he said while kissing me.

"Okay and I'm sorry that I forgot to make the reservations for your birthday."

"Don't worry you can make it up to me when I get back."

"Okay."

I waited until I was sure that he was gone and then Kiera and I began decorating the house, cooking the food, getting ready, and calling to invite all his family and friends over. At ten o'clock everyone was there waiting in the dark. Ten minutes later we saw some head lights from a car and we all hid and when the door swung open we all screamed.

"Surprise!"

"You little sneaky woman I thought that you said that you didn't have anything planned."

"I forgot."

"I'm sure you did."

He began hugging and kissing me.

"Baby everyone is here."

"Oh yea I almost forgot."

We turned on the music, popped bottles open, started dancing and the party began. Everyone was enjoying themselves even people neither me nor Juelz knew. While everyone else did their thing Kiera pulled me to the side to talk.

"Girl we did it."

"Yes we did at first I thought it was going to be kind of hard to pull all of this together because honestly I can't get anything pass him."

"Speaking of which have you thought about what you want to do and have you told him yet?"

"No and no look Kiera I know it's hard knowing something this big and keeping it a secret but I'm going to get it together because I don't know how much more time I have to make up my mind."

"What do you mean?"

"Girl his mama figured out by just looking at me."

"So is she going to tell?"

"No because I didn't tell her my true thoughts so she promised to keep it a secret."

"You really got to make up your mind very quickly."

"Yea I know but I will be back this baby is pressing on my bladder."

I went to the bathroom and when I came back everything seemed normal except the fact that I saw the girl that I had Caught leaving Juelz house some months back and his friend was nowhere to be found but if that wasn't strange enough Juelz whole face expression changed and he looked very uncomfortable.

"What are you doing here!"

"My friend invited me."

"And who is your friend?"

"Me, myself, and I."

"Well me, myself, and I ya'll better find ya'll way up out of here."

"I will if you dance with me."

"No!"

"Well I guess I'll stay then and see what you trying to hide."

"You need to leave."

"Dance with me."

"Will that make you leave?"

"Yea."

Before they could dance I went to the table.

"Hi welcome to the party I'm Royal Juelz's girlfriend but my friends call me Ro-Ro."

"Hi Royal I'm Carmen."

"Well it's nice to meet you Carmen."

"The same to you, well I'm going to leave and let you finish talking but be sure to enjoy yourself."

"Why are you leaving you just got here?"

"I just feel a little unwelcomed oh but before I leave Juelz I'm pregnant with your baby, oh but you already knew that so I'll just see you in two months," she said pulling her jacket back and exposing her almost fully grown belly.

I gave Juelz the eye and begun walking away, he tried to grab my arm but I snatched it away.

"Oh I'm sorry Juelz and Royal is it."

"Go!"

"Are you mad?"

"Leave now!"

She smirked but she got the message and left. The whole crowd stopped and looked. One of his friends tried to calm him down but he was too hot headed to listen. I turned back to Kiera and acted like my feelings wasn't hurt as if to say you're free to do what you please. I couldn't lie my feelings was crushed and I felt like breaking down in the middle of the party but I was a woman before anything and I was always told that a woman should never fall apart in public.

"So what you going to do?" Kiera asked.

"I'm going to finish this party out and then I'm going to pack up and leave."

"Come on Ro-Ro do you really think that he could do something like this?"

"Well I don't have to think because I remember seeing this same girl leaving his house the week after my birthday."

"Well before you go making decision don't you want to hear his side of the story first."

"Look I don't want to hear his story or his voice and I don't want to talk about it anymore so please just let it go," I said.

"Excuse me miss can I have this dance?" a nice looking brown skin boy asked me.

"Of course," I said.

We got on the dance floor and we begin dancing. I could see Juelz sitting with his crew watching the whole time but I didn't care I danced the night away. At twelve o'clock everyone was almost gone except a handful, but they were on their way out anyway I waited until I got Kiera's attention and I signal for her to come and help me pack my things. We made it upstairs and we pack my things as fast as possible and when we were done I tried to sneak out quietly but that was kind of hard with just Juelz and Siy being the only ones left behind.

"What is all of this, where are you going?"

"I'm going home with my mama where I should have stayed in the first place and I'm going to beg her to take me back in."

"Come on Ms. Royal can we talk about this?"

"We just did now can you please move so I can leave I don't want any problems."

"I'm not going to let you just walk out of my life."

"You didn't care if I was in or out of your life when you fucking Carmen so please just let me leave!," I said crying.

"Bae it wasn't even like that I promise!" he said and then he kissed me and I slapped him so hard that his face began to turn red.

"Don't ever put your lips on me again."

"Please Ms. Royal I love you!" he said hugging me so tight that I couldn't move.

"Get off of me!" I screamed crying while trying to push him away.

"Juelz don't upset her she's pregnant!" Kiera blurted out.

"You pregnant!"

I didn't say anything I just picked up my suit cases and I began walking away he tried to grab my wrist but I snatched away, stormed out, put my bags in the car, and drove off. I pulled up in front of my mama house but I couldn't stomach the look on her face when she said I told you so, so I turned around and I drove to the nearest hotel and I checked myself in for a week. I couldn't believe that Juelz would do something like this to me although he promised and to be honest he was no different than that jerk Flight that he had tried to save me from. I lied down and I cried in silence until I went to sleep and I went into a deep dream. I could see Star walking towards me and she held this beautiful baby girl. She smiled and said.

"Here's your baby would you like to hold her."

I reached my arms out and she place the baby in my arms and she was the most beautiful baby that I had ever seen in my life. I held her so close, she was so warm and I began to cry.

"She's really a blessing not a curse" Star said as she slowly vanished. I woke up and I smiled while tears ran down my face but this time I had mixed emotions hurt from what I had gone through but happy that I could still get a message from my closest friend. I got up and I looked at my phone and I had twenty missed calls and fifteen voice messages. I looked at the time and it was eight thirty in the morning. I ran me a bubble bath, laid back in the tub, and I talked to my baby.

"Well little one obviously your auntie Star knows something that I don't so I'm going to keep you and when you're ready to come out I'm going to read to you, feed you, change you, put you to bed, love you so hard, and teach you things that only I could teach you. We have a long road ahead of us but as long as we have each other we don't need anyone else" I finished bathing and then I checked some of my missed calls but I only seen two calls that was worth returning and that was Kiera's and my mom's but I called Kiera first.

"Hello."

"You called?"

"Yea I went by your mom's house and you weren't there where, are you are you okay."

"I'm fine I'm at a hotel."

"Why a hotel you know you're more than welcomed to come to my house."

"Yea I don't want to be around anyone that has any connections to Juelz and Siy just happen to be one of his best friends."

"That's very understandable but how about we meet somewhere, anywhere and we don't have to discuss last night."

"Okay let me get myself together and I'll call you so we can meet."

"Okay."

I got off the phone with Kiera and I called my mother.

"Hello."

"Hey mama."

"Don't hey mama me, where are you?"

"I'm in a hotel."

"No you are not in a hotel with my grandbaby."

"How do you know that I'm pregnant?"

"Because Juelz stopped by and he told me everything."

"Mama I'm fine."

"No you are not, now what I'm trying to figure out is why you would whether go to a hotel other than coming here?"

"Because I just needed a break."

"Baby you could have gotten a break I'm not going to stress you out."

"I didn't say that mama but I'm not a baby anymore I can take care of myself."

"You're going to always be my baby."

"Mama I didn't mean it like that, look I'm going to get me a job and get back on my feet and we're going to be just fine."

"Royal you can do all of that here, why are you so stubborn?"

"Mama thank you for your offer and I'm not trying to be stubborn but I need to be somewhere Juelz can't find me, look me and the baby will be fine I promise."

"Well tell me what hotel that you're at and I will stop by?"

"I can't do that but I will stop by your house to see you."

"You promise?"

"Yes mama I promise."

"Ok I love you."

"I love you too."

I got off the phone with my mother, called Kiera told her where we would meet, and I hoped in my car and left. Forty-five minutes later I made it to the Chinese restaurant.

"Hey girl," Kiera said hugging me.

"Hey have you ordered yet?"

"Girl please I wasn't going to order anything for your picky pregnant ass."

"I am not picky."

"Ok if you're not picky then why did you turn down those nachos that I ordered at the last restaurant."

"Because they smelled like somebody's foot."

"Yea well you use to love those nachos before you got pregnant."

I just broke down crying in public I couldn't control it any more. Kiera hopped out of her seat and came around to hug me.

"What have I gotten myself into?"

"Come on Royal pull yourself together don't put stress on the baby."

"Kiera he promised, he promised."

"Please Royal you going to make me start crying."

"I gave him all of me."

"I know but everything is going to be alright I promise."

"How could he do this to me, to us."

"Royal you may be over reacting you haven't given him a chance to explain."

"And as long as I'm on this earth he will never get that chance."

"Royal you don't mean that."

"Yes I do I hate him" I laid my head on her shoulder and I cried until I couldn't cry anymore and when I was done Kiera and I went into the bathroom and I cleaned myself up. When I left the restroom I went right back to the table ordered and acted as if everything was ok. After I finished having breakfast with my friend and talking and laughing we hugged each other, promised to keep in touch and parted ways. I got in my car and headed to my mama house and when I made it I checked my make up and took a deep breath before going inside.

"Hey mama."

"Hey baby" she said hugging and squeezing me like she never wanted to let me go.

"What you doing?"

"Sitting here waiting for you, are you hungry, you want something to drink."

"No thank you mama I had some Chinese food."

"No you can't be feeding my grandbaby all the nonsense you got to give him/her some soul food, it ain't nothing like soul food it touches the soul."

"Mama that was my first time eating some since I been pregnant."

"I hope so I don't need the baby coming out speaking in another language."

"(laughing) that can't happen you just have a big imagination."

"You don't know and I don't want us to be the first ones to find out."

"Ok mama I will take your words into consideration."

"So how are you holding up?"

"I'm fine I guess."

"Royal you need to come home so that I will know that you and the baby are alright I don't need you sitting inside of that small hotel room stressing you and my grandbaby out."

"It's not small."

"It's smaller than a house or an apartment so it's small."

"Mama just go ahead and get it over with go head and say I told you so."

"I'm not going to say any of that and the reason being is because when Juelz came over here I could really tell that he loves you."

"He don't love me and I don't love him."

"Baby you don't mean that you're just a little upset."

"A little upset is an understatement ma he hurt me," I said crying.

And for the first time my mama didn't say anything she just held me like when I was a little girl and I would get a boo boo from hurting myself outside and she held me until I stopped crying and I hugged her back as tight and loving as she was holding me. After talking and being consoled by my mama I hugged her goodbye. When I got outside to get into my car Juelz hopped out of his car and began walking towards me. I hopped in my car and locked all the doors.

"Come on Ms. Royal please talk to me," he said beating on the window.

"Go away leave me alone!"

"Baby please I love you I can't live without you!"

"Come on Juelz you're stressing out the baby," I said crying.

"Ms. Royal I just want to talk," he said calmly with his hands on the window.

I turned my head away from him because I couldn't stand to look at his face.

"Juelz please just leave me alone."

Chapter 13

My mother saw what was going on and she came outside and politely asked him to leave. He hopped in his car and he drove off, I waited at least thirty minutes before I turned my car on to leave. Two and a half months had passed by and I'd kept in contact with everyone with the exception of Juelz. He'd done a paternity test and found out that the baby wasn't his but I didn't care I didn't want anything to do with him. I'd secretly been meeting up with Portia and Marie so that they would know that me and the baby was fine but honestly I could care less if he thought that I was dead. I wasn't over him but I was over the crying. I'd gotten a job and I was a manager at a clothing store. I woke up at eight thirty in the morning and got ready for work. While combing my hair my phone began to ring

"Hello."

"What you doing fat mama."

"Really Kiera."

"Ok I'm sorry big baby."

"For your information I'm not fat I'm just juicy and I'm getting ready for work why what's up?"

"Well you know that I'm having a barbeque tonight."

"Is he going to be there?"

"I don't know but I can make sure he doesn't come."

"No I don't want to do that him and Siy is best friends just save me a plate and I'll get it tomorrow."

"No Royal you're my best friend and you never come to my get togethers."

"I know and I'm sorry but I'm going to show up one day."

"Royal!"

"Ok, ok I'll stop by after work but as soon as I see him I'm leaving."

"Ok thank you, bestie."

"Yea, yea, yea what are friends for."

I got off the phone with her and I left to go to work. I went to work with a smile on my face. The day was going well and I really liked the place that I worked. Everyone was friendly and you always met new people and as if the devil walked through the door and hopped on my back himself Carmen and her home girls walked through the door. They looked up and saw me and they smirked.

"I bet her and Juelz ain't no strong couple now with her stuck up ass," they said laughing.

I wanted so badly to curse them out but my job was more important than their stupidity.

"Girl I'm glad that my baby ain't Juelz because if he was I would be walking around looking just as stupid as her," Carmen said.

"I know that's right" her friends agreed.

"Do you ladies need help with anything?" one of the workers asked them.

"Na'll we were just looking around but we don't see anything special so we just going to leave" They walked out laughing

I finished working and then I stopped by Kiera's house like I promised

"Oh look at you, you look so beautiful," Kiera said as she hugged me

"Thank you and I told you that I was going to show up."

While in the middle of our conversation Siy came over.

"What's up Royal you growing fast?"

"What's up Siy and don't remind me that my beautiful figure might be gone?"

"Girl please if it leaves trust and believe it's going to come back," Kiera said.

"I hope so."

"Girl it will now come on in here and fix yourself a plate" I went inside the house and I fixed me a plate and I came back outside and sat next to Kiera.

"Girl you wouldn't believe what happen to me today!"

"What happen!"

"I was in the store working and in walked Carmen with her home girls and they were saying slay remarks under their breath."

"Girl you should have called me I would have came and put those sluts in their place!"

"Girl why waste my time on them when I got a job that I worked so hard to get, girl please they can have that because at the end of the day I got to make sure that me and my baby is good."

"And that's why I said that I would have slapped them because those people don't know that I know you."

"Girl you are a mess."

"Yes I know," she said laughing.

"Anyways what you been up to?"

"Nothing much but you know that I'm taking up law."

'No girl I didn't know that but congratulations."

"Thank you, look why don't you come in and enroll yourself in school it's not too late."

"Girl I don't know that's going to be kind of hard considering that I'm pregnant."

"It won't be I promise, I can help you from time to time, you know your mama is going to help, and honestly you know that Juelz and his family would break their neck to be a part of the baby's life."

"His family is fine but I don't want anything to do with him."

"Come on Royal you can't keep him away from his child."

"I can and I will."

"Look baby girl I know that you're hurt but don't hurt the baby trying to hurt him in the process, look I know you better than that and this is not you"

"I just want him to feel my pain."

"Believe it or not he's already doing that."

"What do you mean?"

"He's not doing anything that he was doing since you left him, he misses you."

"Well I don't miss him."

"Are you sure?"

"I'm positive, but anyway I'm off tomorrow so what do you want to do."

"I don't know whatever you want to do."

"How about we go to the movies?"

"Just you and me."

"No you, me, Siy, and Rome."

"Who is Rome Miss thang?"

"He's someone that I've been seeing for a month"

"Well I'm happy for you and everything but how do you think that Siy would look at me if I asked him that?"

"Well he may be a little uncomfortable but he's going to go because he loves you."

"I know but do you think that this is a good idea."

"Look I know that Juelz and Siy are best friends but don't cut me out."

"Alright, alright I'll convince him to go because I do need to see who my niece or nephew may be around."

"Thank you."

"Yea, yea, yea you're welcome."

I stayed and talked a little while longer and then I called it a night and went back to the hotel. The next morning, I woke up and I went apartment shopping. I didn't want to go alone so I invited my mama to go with me. I'd seen two apartments already but they were not up to my standard but I was determined to keep looking because I was sure that something was going to come up sooner or later.

"So what part of town are you trying to move in?"

"I don't know somewhere close to my job and close to the school that I'm thinking about attending."

"Oh sweetie you're going to college."

"I'm thinking about it."

"Oh I'm so happy for you!"

"Thank you."

We drove around going to a couple of more apartments but they were a lost call so I called it a day. I dropped my mom off at home went back to the hotel and got ready for my date. While doing my make up my phone began to ring.

"Hello."

"Hey bae I'm ten minutes away from you."

"Okay I'll be ready when you arrive."

"Okay."

I got off the phone and I finished my makeup and I double checked to make sure that my hair was in place. Ten minutes later I was in the car heading for the movies.

"So are you sure that your friends are going to like me?" Rome asked.

"Yes why would you ask me that?"

"Because you said that your best friend boyfriend is the best friend of your baby daddy."

"I know but Siy is really a cool guy."

"I hope so."

And so did I. thirty minutes into the ride we pulled up to the movie theaters and I could see Kiera and Siy waiting next to the ticket booth for us.

"Hey Kiera, Hey Siy," I said hugging them.

"Hi," they said.

"This is Rome, Rome this is my Best Friend Kiera and her lovely boyfriend Siy."

"It's nice to meet you Rome", Kiera said.

"It's nice to meet you too," he replied

"Okay what movie we came to see let's get this over with," Siy said in an agitated voice.

"I want to see Annabelle," I said.

We went and got our tickets, got some snacks, and we went to find our seats. The movie lasted for a good hour and a half but it was great. When the movie was over we stood outside chatting a little bit when we were interrupted by Siy's phone.

"Oh excuse me I got to take this call it's my best friend Juelz," he said.

"Look I'm so sorry about that, we're about to go home but I'll call you later," Kiera said.

"It's okay and I'll be waiting for your call," I responded.

We parted ways. For a minute we rode in silence and then Rome broke the ice.

"So I get the feeling that Siy doesn't like me that much."

"You just have to give him time to warm up to you he's really a cool guy but over all I enjoyed myself."

"I enjoyed myself too because I was with you."

He drove me back to the hotel and he walked me to the door.

"Okay so I'll call you when I make it home".

"Okay."

I close the door and five minutes later it was a knock at my door.

"Did you forget something, Juelz what are you doing here?"

"I miss you."

"Please go away and leave me alone!"

I tried to close the door but he had his foot in the way.

"Ms. Royal don't do this!"

"Don't call me that and what do you want!"

"I want you Ms. Royal." he said walking up to me.

"I'm going to scream!"

"Scream then," he said kissing on my neck.

"Why are you doing this?"

"Because I miss you," he said as he kissed me on my lips and neck and slowly undressed me.

"You look so beautiful," he said slowly laying me on my back while kissing and licking me all over my body.

"Juelz please!"

"I want you so bad," he said kissing me from my belly, to my thighs, then going down to taste my wetness.

"Juelz!"

I felt a rush and my body began shaking, he came up and then he entered me and for the first time I cried not because he was hurting me but because I loved him and the old feelings came back. I wanted so badly to slap and punch him but this feeling felt so good. We made love for hours until we both climaxed and he held me.

"Why did you do it, why did you break my trust."

"Baby I'm sorry I messed up."

"But you promised me, you promised me that you would never do it."

"I know and I'm sorry."

"You looked me straight in my eyes and you lied to me."

"I couldn't stomach losing you."

"So had she not showed up you would have kept it a secret."

"No I was going to tell you."

"When?"

"I don't know, when I felt it was the right time."

"The right time was when I asked you."

"I didn't want to lose you."

"You already did, get out!"

"Ms. Royal."

"Get out!," I said crying.

"I'm going to respect your wishes and leave but I'm not letting you go that easily, I'm going to keep coming back until you take me back."

He walked out and I couldn't do anything but cry. Why was love so hard, why couldn't it be like the romantic movies that I saw on television. I loved him with all my heart but he had betrayed my trust. While sitting in the middle of the floor crying my phone began ringing. I looked at it and it was Rome. I couldn't even answer the phone because honestly I was no different than Juelz. I needed some time to myself because I was so confused and everything was going wrong. That night I turned on the television and I just stared at it until I fell asleep. I woke up the next morning ordered me something to eat and I stayed in the bed most of the whole day but eventually I had to get up because I had a doctor's appointment. After taking a bath, doing my hair, and fixing my makeup I called Kiera to see if she would like to come alone for the ride and of course she was all for it. I went and picked Kiera up and we rode in silence half way there but Kiera could tell that something was wrong so she was the first one to break the ice.

"Hey I'm sorry about yesterday and how Siy was acting."

"It's okay."

"Okay you've been acting strange since I got into the car so are you mad at me for something."

"No I'm sorry I just got a lot on my mind."

"Okay what happened?"

"Last night after Rome dropped me off at the hotel I got a knock at the door and I thought it was him coming back but it turned out to be Juelz."

"What did he do, did he hurt you!"

"No, we made love."

"So are you guys back together?"

"See that's the thing that I'm so confused about, I mean being with him brought those old feelings back and I can't lie I love him with all my heart but every time that I see him I see her and I don't know if I could ever forgive him."

"Do you even know what really happen between the two of them?"

"No and I don't think that I want to know because I don't know if I can listen to it without feeling so much hate towards him."

"Well do you want to be with him?"

"I do but I don't think that the love and the trust that I had for him will ever be the same."

"Well I can't blame you for that but honestly I think that it would be best if you guys sat down and talk."

"I'm not ready."

"Well whenever you are ready because if you truly love this man and you really want to be with him communication is key."

I was happy that I brought Kiera with me because we could talk about anything and she knew how to brighten your day up. We finally made it to the doctor's office and he called me to the back.

"Hi Ms. Wilkinson how's everything going today."

"It's going well."

"Well that's great but I'm going to need for you to lay back on the bed so that I can measure the baby and make sure that he or she is growing properly."

I laid back on the bed and let the doctor examine me.

"Okay so the baby is growing perfectly fine so I will be seeing you again in a couple of weeks."

"Okay."

I got my paper work and I left the doctor's office, dropped Kiera off at home, and I stopped by my mama house. When I made it inside she was so happy to see me.

"Hey baby."

"Hey mama, what you doing?"

"Waiting on Ronald to come back from the store with my season and salt"

"Oh so you in the kitchen throwing down."

"You know that's what I do, so are you going to stay for dinner."

"Yea I can stay I don't have no place to be."

"So how's everything going?"

"Everything's good I guess."

"What do you mean you guess?"

"Juelz came over the other night unannounced."

"Did you guys talk?"

"I wouldn't say we talked but one thing led to another and let's just say that it brought a lot more confusion into my life."

"And why is that?"

"Because I was dating this guy name Rome."

"Is he nice and why haven't I met this guy?"

"Yes he's nice and honestly the reason why you haven't met him yet is because I'm not sure where I'm heading with this."

"What do you mean?"

"That means that I like him, but I can't get Juelz off my mind so half of the time when we're on a date I'm thinking about Juelz, he's just everywhere."

"It sounds like to me that you're in love with one guy and using the other one as a rebound."

"I'm not using him as a rebound."

"Well what would you call it then?"

"Finding myself."

"Well while you're finding yourself Rome is thinking that you guys have something that you don't have."

"Well I'm trying to get Juelz out of my head."

"Well like the old saying goes the heart can't help who it loves."

"I could be the first."

"Well, baby girl you're doing a terrible job."

"Thank you mama."

"I'm just being honest."

"Anyways enough about me how are things going between you and Ronald."

"Everything's going well he's really nice but the only problem that I have with him is his job."

"Why is that?"

"Because he's always away on business so I barely get to see him but he said that I'm going to be seeing him more now because everything is going to be happening here."

"Well that's good at least one of us has our love life figured out."

"Don't worry baby girl soon all the pieces are going to fall in place like they say whatever is meant to be it's going to be rather you like it or not"

"I guess"

While my mom and I were having a conversation Ronald walked in.

"Hey lady!"

"Hey Ronald."

"So what wind blew you on over here?"

"The one that keep me guessing and wondering about my life."

"Awww girl it's just a little blizzard things will get better in no time."

"Well I hope so because my plate is full."

"Speaking of a full plate I hope you have an empty stomach because I threw down in the kitchen," mama said.

"Mama I will always have some space for your food."

"I hope so because I won't be accepting any excuses."

Chapter 14

I enjoyed dinner with my family then I returned to my hotel room. The next day I went apartment shopping again only to come across to this nice condo that I couldn't resist it was a two bedroom enough for my baby and I, it had a family room, a living room, a nice size kitchen, a big back yard, a walk in closet, and two big bathrooms with a garden tub, not that it would make any difference to the baby but it most definitely made one to me. I picked up the phone and I called the number that was on the sign.

"Hello Sarah Telle's speaking."

"Yes I was passing by this beautiful condo and it caught my eye and I was trying to find out how much are you looking for"

"Well I'm looking for seven hundred dollars a month with no bad credit, so how does that sounds"

"That's sounds great listen I'm trying to move in as soon as possible so how soon can you meet me"

I can meet up with you, now if you like"

"That will be great"

"Ok I'll be there in twenty minutes"

"Sounds like a plan"

I got off the phone and I was so excited although it had taken long enough I was finally getting on my feet and not because of someone else's money. After waiting for almost twenty minutes Sarah finally showed up, we did a walk through and I couldn't wait to sign the papers but not before I got approved and when she left the first thing I did was called my home girl Kiera.

"Hello."

"Girl I have a surprise for you."

"What is it?"

"Now you and I both know that it wouldn't be a surprise if I told you, so I'm going to text you an address and I would like you to meet me there."

"Okay."

I got off of the phone with Kiera and half an hour later she showed up.

"Girl what in the devil is this/"

"This my friend is going to be my new home."

"Really?" she said very excited.

"Yes I mean I haven't got approved yet but I'm very confident that I will get it"

"You will, oh my god Royal I'm so proud of you?"

"Thank you and now I will be able to have dinners over my house."

"Well I better be the first one to be invited."

"Don't worry you will be one of the first ones to know."

The next couple of days I went back and forth to work waiting on this lady to call and approve me of the condo. While on my way to work I notice a car behind me following that I hadn't noticed before. I tried to see through the window but they were tinted I felt like it was Juelz so I pulled into a shopping center and when I parked they parked three lots down from me. I hopped out of my car and run towards their car and they drove off. This was one of the strangest days that I had ever had in my life when I was sure that the car was gone I hopped in my car and I headed to work when I made it inside my coworker noticed something different about me.

"What's wrong?" she asked.

"Nothing I just thought someone was watching me from a far."

"Did you see anyone?"

"No."

"Well maybe it's just the baby that's making you jumpy."

"Yea maybe."

I didn't have the courage to tell her that I saw someone following me because I wasn't quite sure myself. I put my things up and I began working and again I noticed the same car so instead of taking the front way out so that they can spot me I took the back way out and I snuck up on them and to my surprise it was.

"Terri?"

"Oh my god I'm so sorry," she said.

"What are you doing here?"

"I'm sorry I just wanted to see you I know that you're upset with me but."

"Terri I've been looking for you since the night of Star's death."

"I'm so sorry I just had to get away after I got Star killed I just couldn't live with myself."

"Stop it nobody got Star killed, look would you like to come inside?"

"No I don't want to disturb you at work."

"Well how about we meet up after I get off."

"Really?"

"Yea, you, Kiera, and I."

"Are you sure that Kiera would like to see me?"

"I'm positive look how about we exchange numbers."

"Okay."

We exchanged numbers and I went back to work I couldn't believe that Terri had managed to hide out for that long abandoning not only her friends but her family. I must admit that I wasn't quite the best friend in the world at that time but when you go through something you need someone to blame for it other than yourself. I finished work and then I called Terri and asked her to meet me at the hotel and then I called Kiera I didn't tell her why I was calling other than I needed to show her something at the hotel I didn't need to tell her because if I knew Kiera as much as I thought I did then I knew that she would be just as excited as I was. At eight o'clock Kiera showed up at the hotel and we talked a little bit but then she began to get impatient.

"So where is this thing that you had to show me?"

"Don't worry it'll be here in a minute."

"Hold on wait a minute is it Juelz."

"No."

"Well I don't want to meet anyone else look I'm sorry I know that my loyalty is with you but I'm also friends with Juelz so I can't betray him anymore I did it once and he made me feel so bad about it."

"First of all it's not a guy and secondly you were my friend first so what do you mean you don't want to betray him anymore."

"Royal I know that I'm your friend so I have to be loyal to you first but I like Juelz and you never even heard him out to hear the real story."

"That's because there would have never been a story if he really cared about me like he said."

"Okay I understand but can we please get off this conversation I don't want to argue I just want to know what you have to show me."

In the middle of our conversation someone knocked on the door.

"Okay take a seat I have to get the door."

Kiera sat down and I went to answer the door and when the both of us returned to the living room Kiera was in shock.

"Terri is that you?"

"In the flesh."

"Where have you been?"

"I was going to tell Royal that but it's good that we're all here."

Terri and I sat down and she began to tell her story.

"On the night that Star passed away I was just so distract because I felt like it was my fault I just wanted to disappear so I hopped in my car and started to drive I didn't know where I was going and I didn't care I mean it wasn't like anyone would miss me, anyway I ended up in Albany, Ga and I cried myself to sleep in my car. The next morning, I woke up to someone tapping on my window and it was an older lady she was in her late thirties and she asked me why was I sleeping in my car and I told her that I was running from someone and she asked me who and I told her that I was running from myself.

"Now what could you have possible done that was so bad for you to run from yourself?"

"I don't want to talk about it."

"Well that's fine but that won't stop me from sitting here, now where do you live?"

"A long way from here."

"Well come on inside and get you something to eat."

"I'm not hungry."

"Now look girl you look like you could be around the same age of my daughter so that would make you eighteen or nineteen but either way you're still someone's baby and I refuse to leave you out here by yourself for the hungry wolves to get so get your butt out of this car and follow me inside now".

I sat there just thinking for a while because I didn't know this woman she could do anything to me but then again I didn't care I didn't deserve to live anyway so I followed her inside, her home was so warm and homely. I followed her to the kitchen and I took a seat.

"What do you want to eat?"

"Nothing."

She gave me one of the meanest looks that I had ever seen in my life.

"Okay I guess I'll have an egg and bacon sandwich."

"Now that's more like it, look I don't know what kind of trouble that you have gotten yourself into and I don't care as long as you keep it outside of my house but if there is any time that you would like to talk about it I'm here to listen."

"Thanks I'll remember that."

She gave me a room in her big five-bedroom house and for a month straight I stayed in that room doing nothing but crying, I couldn't sleep, I couldn't eat, and I could barely shower and then one day she bust in my room and said.

"That's it I will help you as much as I can but you're not going to sit around here moping all day and night now you going to have to get up get a job or go to school but there will be no slackers in this house."

"Well I'll just go back to my car," I said as I started to get up.

"You will do no such thing!"

"Yes I will I'm grown I make my own decision I don't need you, I don't need anybody I got everything I need."

"What do you have besides yourself"?

"That's all I need"

"Baby girl I don't know what it is that you're going through…."

"That's right you don't know so just leave me alone," I said and I stormed out the house and I got in my car and I broke down crying but she wasn't done with me just yet.

"I don't know what you're going through but whatever it is confess it to god because even if you have no one else in your corner you'll always have god, now there's a church right down the street that I attend every Sunday I will be there tomorrow if you would like to attend god bless you child" she said and she walked off that night I cried so hard that I fell asleep and I didn't remember how but I had a dream and Star walked out of this bright light and told me to open my heart to god. It was so real so real that I woke up and cried. At nine thirty that morning I got up I didn't have a shower or anything and I didn't care. I got out of my car and walked down the street and I entered the church and I sat in the very back and I listen to the pastor preach. At the end of him preaching he asked if anyone wanted to come to the front and be prayed for I went to the front, got on my knees, cried, let the pastor pray for me, and I asked god to forgive me. Although I hadn't quite opened up I felt a little better so the first thing I did when I left church I went and knock on the lady door to apologize and surprisingly she opened the door so that I can come in and I followed her to the kitchen and we sat down. And before I could think I just blurted it out.

"I got my friend killed."

"What!"

I began to tell her everything what happened and at the end of my story she said.

"That's not your fault you girls are young you're going to make mistakes that's just life but you never miss the consequences of what you do."

"But it's my fault I'm the reason why she's dead and that's why I lost everyone."

And she just looked at me with tears in her eyes and she began telling her story "When I was around your age I had my first daughter and I named her miracle because to me that's what she was because before she was ever born or even thought about I grew up without any parents I grew up in an orphanage and I was determined to find my parents and tell them just how I felt about them abandoning me but along the way I got caught up in drugs, alcohol, and a very abusive relationship, I became a stripper, and after that a prostitute, I owed people and not just anybody dangerous people, and then I became pregnant and I decided that I didn't want that life anymore that I would do right by my child. So I went and stayed with a friend I got a job and my baby had everything that she could possibly want, at the same time that I was pregnant my friend was too so we had our babies around the same time, they even started their first day of school together. One day while I was at work my friend kept my daughter and although it was a school day she was scheduled to pick them up after school but my pass came to haunt me and the people that I owed had something else in mind they went to the school and kidnapped her, raped her, and stabbed her fifty times. My friend went to school looking for the girls but her daughter was nowhere to be found, they found her body in a ditch, they killed the wrong girl!" she said crying.

Chapter 15

"They arrested the guys three days after the murder, but that wouldn't bring my friend's daughter back. My friend was depressed for two months straight I had tried to apologize in so many ways but it wasn't good enough and one day she just couldn't take it anymore so she locked herself in the bathroom and she blew her brains out holding her daughter picture. When my daughter got old enough to figure out what had happened she never forgave me so she did everything in her power to get away from me, she went to school graduated, and went to Michigan state college and I haven't heard from her in a year, talking about losing everyone you ever loved, they were all I had, they were all I had" she said breaking down crying. The next day I went back to the church I told the pastor my story and he prayed for me. I got up off my butt, went and got myself together, and I got me a job, every now and then I would follow you guys around and see what you were up too but I couldn't show my face because I was afraid that you would never forgive me."

"Well, forgiveness has to come from all three sides, we all made a crazy decision and if I could turn back to hands of time then we would all be sitting on this couch right now," I said.

"I agree, we're not perfect we're just young and we needed someone to blame but I'm willing to give this thing another try because I'm sure that's what Star would want," Kiera said.

"Me too," Terri said and we all hugged we stayed up all night talking and catching up and the next morning I finally got the call that I had been waiting for and I couldn't help but to scream to the top of my lungs.

"What?" Kiera asked.

"I've been approved."

"Congratulations!" Kiera and Terri said.

"Thank you but first I got to go sign these papers and get my key and then we're going furniture shopping."

"Okay," they said.

And I did just that I went to the lady office, signed the paper work, and then I got my key. My girls and I went to the furniture store and we got everything from the kitchen to my bedroom but I wasn't going to decorate the baby's room yet until I found out the sex. When we were sure that we had everything we went back to the house and brought it alive and when we were done not only had my condo came together but so had we and I just wanted to cry thinking of all the old times. For the first night in the house the girls spent the night with me. The next day we all got up for work and/or school and we hugged each other goodbye and promised to set another day to get together. When I made it to work I just couldn't get the smile off of my face.

"Okay who is he?" my coworker Linda asked.

"Nobody I got approved and moved into my condo yesterday."

"Well, congratulations I'm so proud of you."

"Thank you but after last night I'm so exhausted I can't wait to get home so that I can get me some rest."

"Girl you better get all the rest you can because when the baby comes you'll barely receive any of that."

"I know right."

I began working and just as the day had begun it seemed like it had ended just as fast well almost, anyway it was time for me to go home but it was pouring down and I didn't have an umbrella so as fast as I could I ran and got into my car. I started the car and I pulled off I was so excited that I couldn't wait to get home and just in a blink of an eye a car came and slammed into me and I blacked out. When I opened my eyes I was in a hospital bed and everyone was standing over me.

"What happened, where am I?"

"You was in a car accident and you're in the hospital," Kiera said.

"My baby what about my baby?"

"The baby is just fine you just have a broken leg," Terri said.

"How long have I been here?"

"Two days," Juelz said.

"What are you doing here?"

"I'm here to take you home."

"Oh no you are not where is my mom?"

"She's out of town listen Royal I got to go to school and Terri has to go to work and they will not discharge you without someone that's going to help you," Kiera said.

"But him out of all people."

"Come on Royal we're going to check on you every day you're in good hands trust me," Kiera said.

"We're going to see you later we love you," Terri said.

"I love ya'll too."

When they left I sat in the room quiet the whole time and an hour later the doctor came in with my discharge papers

"Okay so I will discharge you in the care of ...."

"Juelz her boyfriend," Juelz said.

"Ex-boyfriend," I said.

"Okay ex-boyfriend Juelz will you be available until she is well enough to take care of herself."

"Yes I'm free twenty-four hours a day."

"Ok so I'm going to need you and Ms Wilkinson to sign these papers."

We signed the papers and soon I was being wheeled to Juelz car. He picked me up, put me in the passenger seat, put my seat belt on, closed my door and proceeded to the driver's seat. He put on his seat belt and started the car. I looked out the window the whole time until I noticed that we were in front of his house.

"What are you doing?"

"Taking you inside the house."

"Why?"

"So that I can take care of you until you get well."

"Why couldn't I stay at my home?"

"I mean we can if you give me the address but I'll still be there every day."

I didn't say a word.

"I thought so."

He got out of the car, got my will chair out the trunk of the car, got me out of the car and put me in my wheel chair. When we made it inside the house he sat me in a recliner chair in the living room.

"What would you like to eat?"

"I'm not hungry."

"Soup it will be I'm sure the baby would like that."

He went inside the kitchen and warmed up some soup and brought me a bowl, crackers, and orange juice.

"Is this warm enough for you?"

"I said I'm not hungry."

"Well I guess I'll just have to feed you."

"Okay I got it myself I'm not handicap."

"Okay I'll come and check on you in a minute," he said as he disappeared upstairs and when he came back down my bowl was empty.

"Okay your room is ready."

"I will not be sleeping upstairs I prefer to stay here."

"Okay if that's what you want" he turned on the television and disappeared once again upstairs and after a while of watching television I dozed off and when I woke up the next morning I was in the guest room, lying in the bed in one of his big t shirts.

"Good morning sleepy head how did you sleep?"

"How did I get up here?"

"I carried you, now what do you want for breakfast because you have to take your medicine."

"Nothing."

"Eggs, bacon, biscuit, and orange juice it is."

While he was talking someone rung the door bell.

"I'll be back I have to get the door."

He went down stairs and answered the door and two minutes later Kiera and Terri showed up.

"Good morning."

"Oh look who it is my supposed to be friends."

"Oh stop acting like that Royal I had to go to school and besides Juelz won't do anything to hurt you."

"Wrong he forcing me to eat."

"That's a good thing because you can't be starving the baby," Terri said.

"Shut up!"

"Royal we love you and that's exactly why we couldn't leave you at home fending for yourself and the baby while you're handicap," Kiera said.

"I'm not handicap."

"Well disable," Terri said laughing.

"I see someone that want a cast in their eye."

"Royal stop being mean before you have a mean baby," Kiera said.

"Good and maybe he/she will come slapping ya'll around."

"So what you saying is you want the baby from hell?," Terri said.

"There you go again with the jokes."

"Okay I'm sorry but you know that I work and Kiera goes to school so what would you like for us to do."

"Tell them ya'll going on a six month leave to take care of your pregnant friend with a broken leg."

"So in other words you want me to flunk school and Terri to get fired how selfish."

"That's not what I want at all but I don't want to be here with him either."

"Well too bad you're stuck with me," Juelz said making everyone jump.

"Breakfast is served a cheese and ham omelet, bacon, biscuit, hand sliced fruit, with orange juice," he said and then he left the room.

"Damn girl if you don't want him I sure will take him I would love for a man to serve me in bed," Terri said.

"Girl you would take any man that has two legs and a penis," I said laughing.

"Oh the shade," she said laughing.

"Well we had to come and check on you before we left to take care of business but as soon as we are free we will be back," Kiera said.

"Traitors."

"We love you too," they said and they left.

I ate my breakfast, took my medicine, and I went back to sleep.

Three months had passed by and Juelz had been taking me to my appointments for both my baby and my leg and now I was no longer in a wheel chair but I was now on crutches. I still had managed not to talk to Juelz like he didn't exist. The girls were still checking on me and so was my no good mother who refuse to take me with her claiming that I was in good hands but besides all that my doctor told me that my leg was looking good and it was no guarantee that I would have to deal with this cast for three more months because my leg was healing fast and that was some of the greatest news that I could come by. I woke up and as if I stood up too fast I landed hard on my butt on the floor and once again here was Juelz running to help me up.

"I don't need your help I can get up by myself."

"Well I'm going to help you anyway."

"Why wouldn't you rather be helping Carmen?"

"Look why don't we just talk about this thing right now."

"I don't want to."

"Well I do, I know that we were young when we first started dating but there has never been a time that I didn't know what I wanted so when your mama basically asked you to choose between me or her I left because you shouldn't have had to do that, but you left for a week straight without even contacting me and I didn't know if I would ever speak to you again."

"So you did sleep with her?"

"Royal."

"Did you sleep with her?"

"Listen she came over here talking about her man was treating her like shit saying how he wasn't showing any affection towards her, how he cheated with different woman, and how she had to do herself, she came out of nowhere and started to rub on me, I ain't gon lie we kissed but I stopped her before anything else could happen."

"You son- of- a-bitch!"

"Ms Royal I fucked up but I couldn't risk losing you."

"I hate you!"

"I'm sorry."

"I fucking hate you, please just go away!"

"Ms Royal I love you!"

"Leave or I'll leave!"

"Okay, okay you got it"

He walked out of the door and when I was sure he was gone I just broke down crying I wanted to hate him so bad but something inside me just loved him so much. I was so confused how, could you hate a man and love them at the same time. I didn't know but I wanted so badly for him to just be my past and for me to start a new beginning. That gave me an idea and I called Rome.

"Hello stranger."

"Hi."

"This is funny because the last time I heard or seen you I was taking you out to the movies and meeting your friends."

"I know and I'm sorry but there were some things that I had to figure out."

"With your ex."

Silence.

"You don't even have to tell me that because I expected it."

"Are you upset with me?"

"Not really so stranger how about we go out for dinner."

"I would love to but I'm kind of in a broken situation."

"What do you mean?"

"Well three months ago I was in a car accident and I broke my leg."

"Oh wow why didn't you call me I would have been there?"

"Because I woke up two days later confused."

"So how about I come over and bring you some soup?"

"Well I would love that but all of my friends and family were so busy when I got out the hospital so they discharged me in the care of Juelz so I'm kind of stuck at his place."

"Are you guys back together?"

"No!"

"Well I can still come and bring you some soup."

"I don't know Rome, he kind of has a temper."

"I'm not going to come for a fight I'm just going to drop you off some soup now if he asked me to leave his property I will do just that but I just want you to know that I care."

"Okay."

"Oh and by the way when you are healed you owe me a date."

"No problem."

Chapter 16

I sat in bed watching television and talking to my mom and my home girls on the phone after I ended my calls I dozed off and took a nap but that was interrupted by a door bell. I got up hopped on my crutches towards the window and there was Rome holding my soup.

"Can I help you?" Juelz asked.

"No I just came to bring Royal some soup."

"Well she sleeping right now so who do I tell her stopped by."

"You don't have to tell her she already knows who I am."

"Is that right?"

"Yea."

"Well the next time you come by my house she's going to know who you were."

"I don't want any problems I just came to drop this off but you have a good day man."

"Yea you too."

I heard the door close and then Rome looked up at me and waved and I waved back before hopping back to my bed. Two minutes later my door swung open.

"Someone dropped you off some soup?"

"Awww that was sweet."

"So who is he?"

"None of your business."

"Look Ms Royal I get that you're trying to hurt me I do, but for his own sake if you want him to live don't ever let him step foot on my property again."

"Well soon I'll be well and then he'll be stepping all on my property."

"We'll see."

"What is that suppose to mean?"

He didn't say anything he just walked out. The next day my girls were free so they came and picked me up and took me out.

"So what has it been like living with Juelz again?" Kiera asked.

"First of all I'm not living with him I'm just there until I heal and everything is going great."

"Okay I don't like the way you said great, what did you do" Kiera asked

"Nothing Rome just came over to bring me some soup yesterday."

"Royal you didn't," Terri said.

"What do you mean I didn't Juelz and I are not together so I'm entitled to date whoever I please."

"But you know how much Juelz love you," Kiera said.

"He don't love me because if he did he wouldn't have cheated on me."

"Royal I get that you're hurt but you know that Juelz screws ain't tight, okay you keep playing with fire and get burned," Terri said.

"Whatever anyways where are we going?"

"Well since you handicap we going to lobster and grill there for you won't have to get up," Kiera said.

"For the last time I am not handicap and if one of ya'll heifers call me that again you getting a ring around your eye."

"Well, excuse us Ms Sassy," Terri said.

We made it to lobster and grill and I ordered everything that I could possible think of. We talked, laughed, and had fun and when we were done they returned me back to the hell hole and as soon as I opened the door he was up waiting.

"Are you ready to take your bath?"

"I'll bathe myself."

"With one leg."

"I don't care if I had no legs I would bathe myself as long as you don't have to do it."

"Yea why so you can risk falling again and hurting yourself or the baby?"

"You are not bathing me!"

"Look I don't have time to go back and forth with you so you either go willingly are unwilling."

"I choose neither."

Without saying a word, he took me upstairs, stripped me, and put me in the tub of warm bubbly water.

"Now doesn't this feel nice."

I said nothing.

"Well that's okay I'll just bathe you in silence, oh by the way I got some good news my mom is coming into town tomorrow."

"Finally someone that I actually care about can come and keep me company."

"That hurts."

"Well how do you think I felt when I found out that you were screwing Carmen?"

"We didn't have sex."

"Call it what you like but I won't ever forgive you."

For the rest of my bath neither one of us spoke. I could tell that he was hurt but I didn't care because I wanted him to feel the same pain that I felt. When he was done bathing me he dried me off, lotion my body, and he clothed me and he left the room in silence. The next day his mom and her husband showed up and we did a lot of talking and catching up. She talked about her marriage and her new place and I talked about the baby, my new place, my job, and of course I couldn't help but to talk about what Juelz had put me through and I didn't get a nasty reaction back she was just like my second mother and she consoled me. She stayed for a week and we did something different every day but she had to finally leave and to say that I was sad was an understatement. two months had passed and the doctor had finally given me some good news that my cast was coming off. I got up early that morning and Juelz took me to my appointment and when my leg was finally free I was so happy but I could tell that Juelz was nowhere near happy. He took me back to his house and I packed my things so that I could leave. I went down stairs but I couldn't leave without saying.

"Thank you for everything, look we may not be together but we can always be friends."

"I don't want your friendship," hc said and he walked away.

I walked outside put my things in Rome's car and we left. I'm not going to lie I wanted so badly to cry because this was not how I pictured things between us I mean I was pregnant with his son, I was in a relationship with another man, and neither one of our hearts would let go. I wanted to turn around and say I forgive you but who's to say that he wouldn't hurt me again. On my way home Rome stopped by the market, bought some food, took it back to my place, and he cooked me dinner. I was so happy because it took my mind off of Juelz.

"So how was dinner?" Rome ask.

"It was delicious who taught you how to cook"

"Well I could give all my props to my mom but I'd be lying because my grandma taught me."

"Oh so you learn how to do some of that old school cooking."

"Well you know what can I say?"

"Really?," I said laughing.

"Really now throw your little feet on my lap so that I can massage them."

"Now this is how a girl is supposed to return back home."

"Well this is not all I'm doing, I'm going to run you a warm bubble bath and then when you get out I will give you a full body massage."

"Okay Mr. Romantic."

"Just stay here and I'll be back."

I stayed there and he did just what he said he ran me some bath water, gave me a full body massage, and then I fell asleep with him holding me. The next morning, I watched him get ready for work.

"Baby are sure you don't want anything for breakfast?" I asked Rome.

"No thank you just a cup of coffee."

"Coffee coming up."

I went down stairs and I prepared him some coffee before he kissed me goodbye and headed to work. An hour later my door bell rung and when I opened it, it was Kiera and Terri.

"Hey ya'll."

"Hey what you in here doing?" Terri asked.

"Nothing I was just seeing my man off to work."

"Oh is that right?" Kiera asked.

"Yes, it is and why did you say it like that?"

"Oh no reason."

"Yea right anyways what are we doing today since both of ya'll are free."

"Well I don't have anything planned right now but I am having a get together tonight and ya'll are invited," Kiera said.

"Alright can I bring my man?" I asked.

"You can but Juelz is supposed to be there tonight."

"I don't care I will act like he doesn't even exist."

"Oh god," Kiera replied.

"Don't worry I won't ruin your dinner."

"Well since everyone is bringing their man can I bring my love?" Terri asked.

"Wait a minute who is this love that I have yet to meet?" I asked.

"I know right," Kiera said.

"Well you know when I told ya'll that I decided to get myself together."

"Yea," Kiera and I responded.

"Well when I started working at this café he would come in every morning and order the same coffee and he would always be alone so one night I had to close and he stayed there until I closed and he told me that he had been watching me and he liked what he saw and we went on a couple of dates and we've been together every since," Terri said.

"That is so sweet," I said.

"Yes, it is I just love true love, but anyway to answer your question yes you can bring him"

"Alright now we can have a triple date," I said.

"I guess," Kiera responded.

"Well enough about our love life now how about you go and get ready so that we can hit up the mall."

"Okay just give me like five minutes."

I ran upstairs, got dressed, did my make up, and I flat ironed my hair and then I was ready to go."

"Well, excuse me Ms Thang you said five minutes and that was actually thirty minutes," Terri said.

"My bad it took a little longer than I thought," I said laughing.

"Try a lot more than you expected," Kiera said.

"I said my bad now get off of my case ya'll know I'm fat and I don't move at the pace that I use to move at."

"See this is what happens when you lay on your back," Terri said laughing.

"Whatever I was raped."

"Yea sure if rape sounds like yes please take me daddy," Kiera said.

"For the record that is not what I said now let's go before I put the both of you in the head lock."

Chapter 17

We left and we went to the mall. I was so excited because since I had broken my leg it had been a while since I'd been there and you best to believe that I couldn't control myself. Not only did I get a dress for tonight that complimented my curves and my baby bump but I also got some more jeans and other things. But I didn't stop at the mall I got Terri to stop me at the baby store so that I could shop for my baby and by the time I left to go home there was nothing that you could say that he didn't have. As soon as I came through the door I went upstairs to decorate my baby's room and when it was done I couldn't believe that I had done it and I couldn't wait for him to come. Later on that night Rome returned home from work.

"Hey baby how was work?"

"It was great how was your day?"

"Well my home girls came by and we went to the mall and I did a little shopping for the baby."

"Is that so?"

"Yes come on let's go check out his room."

He followed me down the hall and when I opened the door he couldn't believe that I had did it myself.

"Wow this is nice but are you sure that you decorated this?"

"Yes I am."

"You did a great job."

"Thank you but you need to go hit the shower and get ready."

"For what?"

"Because my home girl Kiera is having a get together tonight at her house and she invited us."

"Is your ex going to be there?"

"Does it matter?"

"Yes because I don't want any problems."

"There won't be any problems I promise."

"Okay I guess."

We both got ready for the party. At eight fifty-five we pulled up in front of Kiera's house. We got out of the car and we rang the doorbell but I couldn't help but to notice that Rome seemed a bit nervous.

"Relax," I said.

"Is it that obvious?"

"Yes."

Before I could say anything else the door swung open and it was Siy.

"Hi Siy," I said hugging him.

"Hi big girl how, are you?"

"I'm fine and you?"

"I'm great come on in."

I followed him inside "You remember Rome?"

"Yea what's up?" he said dryly.

"Hi."

"Listen Kiera and the rest of the girls are in the kitchen," Siy said.

"Thank you."

"No problem."

I went inside the kitchen and there were Kiera, Terri, and some more girls that I didn't know.

"Hey ya'll," I said.

"Hey, oh my god you look so beautiful," Kiera said.

"Thank you, everyone this is Rome."

"Hey Rome," everyone greeted.

"Hey everyone."

"Well I know you might feel a little uncomfortable with certain crowds but my father, brothers, and some of my cousin are out on the patio if you would like to hang with some of the guys," Kiera said to Rome.

"Okay thank you and I will do just that."

Rome left the kitchen.

"Thank you girl because Siy wanted nothing to do with him when we walked through the door."

"That's because Juelz is in there."

"Oh really I didn't notice."

"Girl please you know you saw him," Terri said.

"Shut up who asked you?" I asked.

"Hey I was just saying don't get upset with me" she replied.

"You ain't saying nothing now where is your man so that we can finally meet him?" I asked.

"Give me one second."

She disappeared for a little while and when she returned there stood a man about 6'1, caramel skin, a low cut, a nice build, and a nicely line up mustache and beard.

"Everyone this is Ace my boyfriend and Ace these are my friends, Royal and Kiera," Terri said.

"Hey boyfriend Ace," Kiera and I said.

"Hi friends," Ace responded.

"We've heard a lot about you," I said.

"Nothing but good things I hope," Ace said.

"They were only good things believe me and I'm so happy that a good man has come into my friend's life and made her happy," Kiera said.

"Yes and I'm glad that I could be that man but the credit goes to her because she brought joy to my life" Ace responded.

"Well we don't want to hold you up we just really wanted to get the chance to meet this man that has my friend smiling nonstop," I said.

"No problem," Ace said as he kissed Terri and walked out of the kitchen.

"Now that man is a keeper," I said.

"Yes god and he's fine too," Kiera responded.

"Girl now ya'll know all we have are fine men," Terri said.

"That's true with the exception of Flight now he wasn't quite my type," I responded.

"But he grew on you," Kiera said.

"Yea I guess, but what we got planned today because I know that you don't plan on just standing around in the kitchen all night," I said.

"Well actually I have a game of charades, spades, and a game of black jack 21 lined up so we about to have fun."

"This reminds me of when we were younger so what are we playing first," Terri asked.

"I want to play charades first so let's go get everyone gathered up," Kiera said.

We exit the kitchen and we started to call everyone inside.

"Okay attention everyone we're about to start a game of charades so it's going to be the women against the men," Kiera said.

"Do we really have to do this I mean we don't want to have to hurt ya'll little feelings," Siy said.

"Excuse me baby but talk is cheap," Kiera replied.

"It ain't when we got the skills to back it up" Juelz said

"I'm sorry what did you say I couldn't hear you over all of the BS," Terri said.

"So what you trying to call our bluff?" Ace said.

"Yea we calling ya'll bluff," Terri responded.

"Well let's stop talking and get this show on the road," Siy said.

We began playing the game and I was having so much fun that I thought that I was a kid again. We did celebrities, animal, family, friends, and anything else that we could possible think of but I would be lying if I said that the game wasn't close but we beat the men by one point.

"Now what was all that stuff that ya'll was saying," Kiera asked.

"Well actually we let ya'll have that point because that's the type of gentlemen that we are," Siy said.

"Okay so after we have mop the floor with ya'll now it's ya'll let us have that point, ya'll didn't let us have anything ya'll just couldn't keep up," I said.

"Really now you would say something when you only got two right out of the whole game," Juelz said looking at me as if he could see through my dress.

"Well I was trying to give ya'll a chance to catch up but that didn't help, ya'll are just natural born losers," I replied.

"I've always been a winner at everything that I do I just try to give everybody a chance to win at something," he said.

"Yea, yea, yea enough of the small talk lets settle this with spades," Kiera said.

"Okay now we definitely are going to win at spades," Siy said.

"Well choose your partner," Kiera responded.

"You already know that I got to get my boy Juelz," Siy said.

"Well I got Royal," Kiera said.

I took a look at Rome and he gave me the okay so I sat down and we began playing and by the time we got up I was so disappointed because the men beat us by thirty-six points.

"A Juelz you hear that?" Siy asked.

"What?" Juelz asked.

"Nothing it's the sound of crickets," Siy replied.

"Yea what happened to all that loud talking ya'll was doing," Juelz asked.

"We just a little thirsty right now," Kiera replied.

"Oh ya'll want some water or something?" Siy asked laughing.

"Hey, hey, hey don't forget that we live together so you stuck here with me when everyone leaves," Kiera responded.

"Oooooooooh," all the men said.

We continued to talk and laugh and have fun and when it was time to fix the plates I couldn't have walked in the kitchen at a worse time while Juelz and Siy was in the kitchen. I got ready to turn around but Siy stopped me.

"Royal where you going girl get on in here and fix my nephew a plate."

I was a little hesitant but I went ahead and started fixing Rome and my plate and everything was going well until Juelz stood behind me.

"Why you here with that clown you know you don't love him?"

"Why do you care and who are you to tell me who I love?"

"Well first of all I care because I still love you and I know you still love me too" he said rubbing his hand down my back. I got ready to turn around and leave but he grabbed me and kissed me so passionately that chills went down my spine.

"I'm here with my date," I said.

"Don't worry I'm watching the door," Siy said.

"Really Siy you're going to help him?" I asked.

"Hey what are friends for," Siy responded.

"Tell me that you didn't just feel anything when I kissed you," Juelz said.

"Can you move?" I asked.

"Look me straight in my eyes and tell me that you didn't feel anything," Juelz said.

"I didn't feel anything," I lied.

"You just looked me straight in my face and lied."

"What do you know?" I asked.

"I know you and I also know that you using that clown to try and forget about me," Juelz replied.

"Well don't worry because soon there won't be a try," I responded.

"There will always be a try as long as I'm living," Juelz said.

"Excuse me," I asked.

"I told you I always knew what I wanted and that's what I get," he said.

"Look stop chasing me and go chase after Carmen you made your bed now go lay in it, now do I have to leave and come back later or are you going to leave?" I asked.

"I'll leave," he said as he kissed once again but this time tears rolled down my face uncontrollably "I love you Ms Royal" He said and then him and Siy walked out of the kitchen. I fixed the plates and I sat in there a while getting myself together but this was something that I just couldn't shake so instead of me staying and eating I took my plate and left by telling Kiera that I wasn't feeling well. I hugged Kiera and Terri goodbye and I left. On the way home Rome and I rode in silence until he spoke.

"Are you okay?"

"Yea."

"Are you sure?"

"Yea I'm just a little nauseous nothing major to worry about."

"Well that's good to know, what do you say about me making you a hot cup of tea and giving you a full body massage."

"That would be nice."

"Ok."

We finally made it to the house and he did just as he had said. He made me coffee and gave me a full body massage but as he did so he decided to speak his mind.

"You know I like your friends their very nice."

"See I tried to tell you."

"Yea but I seen Juelz flirting with you when we were playing the games."

"He wasn't flirting he was just talking."

"No I'm a man I know what it looks like when a man is flirting and he was flirting but I wasn't worried because I know that I have your heart."

"Well since you know that can we stop discussing him because this is ruining my massage."

"Of course my royal queen."

Chapter 18

The truth of the matter was that Juelz still had my heart, now don't get me wrong Rome was a really nice person and I liked him but my opinion was it would take some time for me to give him what I had given Juelz but like the saying goes love takes time. He continued to massage my body and in the process I fell asleep. The next morning, I woke up to a knock at the door and no Rome. I went downstairs to answer the door and when I opened it there stood Kiera and Terri.

"Hey girl," Kiera said.

"Hey what are ya'll doing here?"

"Oh now it's a problem for us to come over?" Terri asked.

"No it's nothing like that I just didn't know that ya'll was free today," I said.

"Well actually I'm off but the other is just playing hooky," Kiera said.

"Now how are you supposed to get a higher position if you not at work?" I asked.

"Well believe me, you, I'm the best worker there is and one day isn't going to hurt anyone," Terri said.

"So what do you and Rome have planned today?" Kiera asked.

"Nothing I guess because when I woke up he was gone," I said.

"He probably had an emergency," Terri said.

"I don't know but I hope all is well," I responded.

"So did you see how smooth and flirty that Juelz was being?" Terri asked.

"He wasn't the only one that was flirting," Kiera said.

"First of all we were not flirting we were just talking," I said.

"So what really happened last night because I know that you weren't sick?" Kiera asked.

"Well Siy and Juelz held me hostage in the kitchen last night," I said.

"What?" Kiera asked.

"It was nothing like that he was just telling me that he knew that I wasn't in love with Rome, I was just using him as a pond, and that he still had my heart," I told them.

"So was he right?" Terri asked.

"Juelz do have my heart but I believe that if Rome and I spend enough time together getting to know each other then everything will fall into place," I said.

"Royal you can't force something that is not there," Kiera said.

"I can if I keep moving forward and forget all about Juelz," I said.

"What could he have done to you that was so bad?" Terri asked.

"He cheated on me with a girl name Carmen," I said.

"Oh my god how did you find out?" Terri asked.

"Because she showed up at the party pregnant and saying that it was his baby and there's only one way to make a baby trust me I know," I said.

"So did he admit it," Terri asked.

"Partially he claimed that they just kissed and felt on each other but she said that they slept together," I replied.

"But how do you know that she's not lying?" Kiera asked.

"How do I know Juelz not lying I mean if it wasn't for Carmen I wouldn't have even known that anything had taken place and besides I don't care if they just kissed or had sex either way it's the automat betrayal," I responded.

"Is that what he said that he wasn't going to tell you?" Terri asked.

"No he said that he was trying to figure out when the right time was because he didn't want to lose me," I replied.

"Then there you have it," Terri said.

"No there you have nothing because the right time was when I asked him and if he didn't want to lose me he wouldn't have never touched her to begin with," I said.

"Royal how would you feel if you were in his shoes and his mom asked him to choose between her and you?" Kiera asked.

"I don't know but the answer most definitely will not be in another man's arm but anyway I don't want to talk about this anymore so what ya'll have plan today," I asked.

"Well we're going to have a triple picnic date at the park today," Terri said.

"Excuse me are you trying to outdo me?" Kiera asked.

"I'm not trying I already have so are ya'll coming?" Terri asked.

"Yea I am," I said.

"I guess," Kiera said.

"Don't be a hater all of your life," Terri said.

"I'm hardly a hater," Kiera responded.

"If you say so but today we're just going to relax and have fun so wear something comfortable don't come looking like you going to a prom or you going to church," Terri said.

"I know that's right Royal," Kiera said laughing.

"Excuse me I do not over dress," I defended myself.

"Now don't get me wrong you do have some nice clothes and when we went to parties we shut everybody down but you do tend to go looking like you going to a Royal ball and that's what Caught Juelz attention," Terri said.

"Well my name is Royal," I responded.

We sat and talked for a couple of hours before we parted ways. I then went upstairs to get dressed and then I stopped by my mother's house. When I arrived she was so excited to see me.

"Hey baby how have you been?" mama asked.

"Hey mama I been fine," I said.

"Well don't just stand there bring your big butt on in here," Mama said.

"So what you in here doing?" I asked.

"Nothing I'm just relaxing before I go to work," she said.

"Where is Ronald?" I asked.

"He's upstairs relaxing because he's off today, so what have you been up to?" Mama asked.

"Nothing working and getting prepared for my baby's arrival," I replied.

"So have you figured out the Juelz situation yet?" she asked.

"No and I'm not focusing on it either," I said.

"So have ya'll spoke?" Mama asked.

"Somewhat but mama why does this matter," I asked.

"Because I know you and him still love each other you just have to get over all the obstacles in the road," she said.

"There's nothing for me to get over because I have moved on," I replied.

"With who?" she asked.

"Nobody that you would know," I said. .

"Well I better get to know him if he plans on being around my grandson," she responded.

"Mama I didn't come to talk about this," I said.

"I know you didn't because you like to sweep everything under the rug but you better wake up, open your eyes, and stop fooling yourself because you know that you're still in love with Juelz," Mama said.

"Whatever."

"You responded with two words because you know that it's the truth," she said.

Chapter 19

I sat with my mom talking until it was time for her to leave for work and then I went to the mall to find me a nice summer dress and hat for the picnic and after I was done shopping I went to the food court and bought me whatever I wanted to eat. There was nothing left to do so I stopped by work to see what my coworkers were up to but I didn't stay because I had easily gotten bored. I finally returned home took me a shower and I took a nap. When I woke up I got dressed, did, my makeup, and then I did my hair but when I was done there were still no Rome. I got ready to reach for my phone to see where he was but then I noticed a note on my pillow that I hadn't notice before and so I picked it up and read it:

"Dear Royal,

In my head I pictured this going differently but I guess it doesn't get any easier. Getting to know you has been everything. You are a nice and caring person and I couldn't have found anyone better that I would like to spend the rest of my life with but the fact of the matter is that your heart belongs to another and it doesn't matter how hard I try that won't detour you because the heart can't help who it loves. Please don't get it wrong I'm not upset with you and this is not the last of me, we can always be friends but what you had with Juelz is what I am looking for in my relationship and you can't give me that not just now but ever. I hope that you and Juelz figure things out because you seem like a really great couple and soon to be family I really wanted to tell you this personally but then it would have been even harder for me to let go. Anyway I don't want to waste your time any longer but I hope you find your way.

Love always

Rome

I couldn't believe it my jaw just dropped I had did everything to forget about Juelz but unfortunately not only could I not lie to myself but I couldn't lie to anyone else and for that reason I was single again. I wanted to lay down in my bed and forget all about the picnic but I decided against it because even if I was the fifth wheel I could have fun all by myself. I hopped in my car and I drove to the park and when I arrived Kiera and Terri just had to know.

"Where is Rome?" they asked.

"He dumped me," I said.

"What?" Kiera asked.

"Yea he wrote me a letter and he said that he could still tell that I was in love Juelz and for that reason it would be wrong for him to try and stay and force me to love him," I responded.

"Awww," Kiera said unsympathetically.

"You don't have to pretend heifer I know that you are jumping for joy inside," I said.

"Oh I would never," Kiera said sarcastically.

"Well if it makes you feel better you can hang out with Ace and I," Terri said.

"Oh no you know I can't do that now ya'll go sit down and enjoy ya'll time with ya'll men," I replied.

"We can't do that to you," Kiera said.

"Really I'm going to be fine now go over there with your man before ya'll be looking like me," I said laughing.

"Well we're going to keep checking on you from time to time," Terri said.

"I am not a baby now go and have fun before I give each of you one of these," I said raising my two fist.

They went on to enjoy their date and I sat by the pond feeding the ducks. Forty-five minutes later.

"You remember when we first came to this park?" he asked.

I paused for a while because he had startled me.

"Juelz what are you doing here did they call you here as a sympathy date?" I asked.

"Well actually Siy told me that ya'll was having a triple picnic and I came to crash it so it was even better when I found out that you were alone," he responded.

"Well he's gone are you happy now?" I asked.

"I really am," he said kneeling down on one knee.

"What are you doing?"

"Royal I know that I broke your heart by kissing another woman and keeping you in the dark about it and that has been one of the worst decision that I have ever made in my life but if you give me a chance to make it right not just for now but for a life time you will not regret it so what do you say you do me the honors of being my wife?" he asked.

And at the moment I had held in all that I could hold and I just broke and tears began falling down my face.

"Juelz you hurt me how am I supposed to get passed something like that."

"I know that it's going to take some time but all I'm asking you to do is to take this chance with me and let's get over it together," he said.

I said nothing I was so confused.

"Ms Royal please I will not hurt you I promise you if you give me your heart I'm going to treat you like the queen that you are and at no time when we are having problems will we go to sleep without making them right. Baby I want you to know that you're the one that holds the key to my heart and I'm not focusing on anything but you and my son. Ms Royal I have jump through hoops trying to get to this point and if you say yes I promise you baby nothing else will come between us unless god calls one of us home so what do you say?" he asked.

"Yes," I said.

"Yes!" he asked surprisingly.

"Yes." I responded

We began kissing but this time as the tears rolled down my face I thought about my future that I would finally have with the man that I loved. He wiped the tears away from my face and he placed the ring on my finger.

"I got you baby there ain't no need for tears," he said.

"Forever?" I asked.

"Forever, but I have one more surprise," he said as he run to the car and came back with a basket.

"What is this?" I asked

"I thought that you might be hungry so I made it my business to make you some finger sandwiches and some fruit. I thought about bringing some wine but I don't want my baby brains to turn upside down," he replied.

"Really his brain turning upside down?" I asked.

"Hey you never know and I don't want my son on the news for being crazy and killing off the whole school," Juelz said.

"You are so silly but this is so nice and romantic," I said.

"Only for you Ms Royal," he said.

We continued with the Picnic and it was the happiest moment of my life. We talked, he fed me fruits, and we laughed. This was a special night because it was like we were getting to know each other all over again. After the picnic we returned to his house and we went into the Theater room and we watched the first movie that we ever watched together. Their Eyes Are Watching God.

"So you mean to tell me that you still remember our first movie that we ever watched together?" I asked

"How could I forget when there was a woman as fine as you sitting right next to me smelling so good," Juelz responded.

"You mean the girl that had you scared to make a move?" I asked.

"I wasn't afraid to make a move but with someone as precious as you I wanted to take my time, my mama once said that something that is worth waiting for is worth having and keeping and I felt like you were that one."

"You didn't know a thing about me so how did you know that I was worth waiting for?" I asked.

"Because I watched you and it was just a feeling I got whenever you were around me," Juelz said.

"So what did you find out by watching me?" I asked.

"I found out that you were a fun, outgoing young lady, you had a sneaky side, but you also had a watchful eye, you were careful, a great friend, and very loving," he said.

"So when were the first time that I made your heart skip a beat?" I asked.

"When I first saw you," he said.

"So you never once looked at anyone of my friends?" I asked curiously.

"No, listen your friends are nice looking women don't get me wrong but when I saw you I was like damn I got to have her. I wanted to talk to you then but I was like walking into a group of women to pull one woman to the side was a no, no, so I waited but as I was getting ready to approach you Flight showed up first now I was a little upset because he knew that I had my eyes set on you but then after I seen that he got your number and everything I let you know that I liked what I saw and I stepped back because I just knew that ya'll wouldn't work out," Juelz responded.

"And how did you figure that?" I asked.

"Because I knew Flight and he wasn't anything nice," he said.

"So why didn't you stop me from dating him?" I asked.

"So you think that if I had tried to stop you that you wouldn't have thought that I was side hating?" he asked.

"No I wouldn't have," I responded.

"That's a lie because the first time that I approached you, you weren't feeling me and I could tell it," he said.

"You would have treated me the same way if every time you turned around it was said that Royal had a new boyfriend," I said.

"That's not true because I don't like to go by rumors I like to find out things on my own," he said.

"So if you heard that I was freaking the streets you still would have wanted to get to know me?" I asked.

"Of course I mean after all I was told that you and your crew was gold diggers and you left men high and dry after you were done using them and I still wanted get know you," he replied.

"Excuse me and just where did you hear this little rumor?" I asked.

"It was just floating around in the streets but I didn't get that kind of vibe from you I just felt like you were very careful with who you dated and that whoever made up the rumor may have gotten turned down before," he said.

"I highly doubt it because I wasn't that good with turning guys down," I replied.

"Well like I said I use to watch you and I have seen a lot of guys get turned down," he said.

"I have not," I said.

"Yes you have and that was another reason that made me want you because I like a challenge and I like things that I can't have," he said.

"So was it worth it?" I asked.

"Well of course I mean do you really think that I will be chasing you like crazy if you weren't worth it?" Juelz asked.

We finished talking and then we headed upstairs where he ran my bath water, rubbed my whole body down with lotion, and held me until I fell asleep in his arms. I woke up the next morning and he was gone. I looked out of the window but his car was nowhere to be found. I didn't want to over react so I sat there, calm trying to figure out where he could possibly be. Forty-five minutes later his car pulled up and when he opened the car door there stood his mother. I hurried and lie down until I heard the door and the stairs.

"Good morning sleepy head," Juelz said.

"Good morning," I responded.

"We have company but mostly you," he said.

"Oh really and who could that possibly be?" I asked.

"Come down stairs and see," he said.

I got up and followed him down stairs and there his mom stood at the bottom of the stairs.

"Hey girl how, are you and my grandbaby doing?" She asked greeting me with a hug.

"Hey Mrs. Marie and we are fine how about yourself?" I asked.

"I'm fine but what did I tell you about calling me Mrs. Marie."

"I know and I'm sorry I just have a habit of doing that but I'm working on it," I said.

"You don't have to apologize for having manners but soon I'm going to be your mom and I don't expect to hear Mrs. Marie all the time," she replied.

"I know and I'm so excited," I said.

"Not as excited as I am, when I heard that you left him and what he had done I told him that whining like a little baby wasn't going to get him anywhere and he needed to go and find you because you were the best thing that ever happened to him," she said.

"Thank you, I feel the same way about him too and that's exactly why I couldn't stomach what had taken place but the worst part is trying to move forward and forget about that person and may I add that it's very difficult," I responded.

"I know the feeling but I'm so happy that you guys are back together because you are his better half," she said.

"That's so sweet, but what I want to know is, are you going to help me to plan my wedding?" I asked.

"Of course I am I'm just so grateful that you asked me!" she said.

"No better way to bond with your soon to be mother in law other than planning a wedding together," I said.

"I hear that and I'm most definitely not complaining," she responded.

"Awww but really thank you so much."

"No problem," she said as she hugged me.

"Ok so the first thing that I would like to look at is the wedding dresses."

"What kind of dress are you looking for?"

"I'm not sure all I know is that I want to look beautiful."

"Well you don't need a dress for that."

"You're so sweet but there's one more thing that I have to tell you."

"What's that?"

"Well my mom will also be helping us to plan the wedding."

"That's great the more the merrier and besides I need to get to know the woman the raised such a smart, respectful, beautiful young lady."

"Thank you so much for all the compliments but if I get any more my head is going to explode."

"Well I can't help it you deserve them, but really thank you for changing my son's life."

"Well your son also changed mine."

"I'm glad to hear that."

"Ok so I have two brides' maids but I wanted to know if Portia would be willing to be the lucky number three."

"Of course Portia would be excited to be a part of the wedding."

"Well let me call and give her the exciting news."

I called Portia and she was so excited to know that she would be one of my brides' maids and so was I. I got off the phone and I began helping Mrs. Marie find my wedding dress and when we were too exhausted to continue looking we called it a night. The next morning, I woke up to breakfast in bed.

"Good morning my beautiful soon to be wife."

"Good morning my handsome soon to be husband."

"Here you are my lady."

"Breakfast in bed what's the special occasion"

"There's nothing more special than the beautiful woman that is in my sight."

"Awww baby that's so sweet and I feel the same way about you but if you keep on doing things like this I'm not going to want to get out of the bed."

"I'll like that."

"Okay now wait until I drop this baby and mama is going to show you how it's really done."

"I can't wait."

We began kissing. The kiss was so passionate that I could taste the sweet flavor of orange juice on his lips.

"I love you baby," Juelz said.

"I love you too."

"So what do you have planned today?"

"Work and then I might check on my girls and see what their up to before I have to meet with both of my mom's to finish making plans for the wedding."

"I love to hear you say both of your mom's because my mom really loves you like her own."

"I know I feel the same way, it's going to be great to have someone else to shop with and talk to when I need a shoulder to lean on."

"But I thought that, that's what I was here for."

"Well you are somewhat but sometimes men don't always understand where women are coming from and besides I can't talk to you about you when you make me mad."

"Oh is that right?"

"Yes that's right."

"Well I'm going to make sure that I keep you happy so that I can never be the topic of your discussion."

"I hope so."

"I know so."

He gave me a kiss and he began to get his things together.

"Where are you going?"

"If I tell you then I will have to kill you."

"I thought that we agreed that there will be no more secrets."

"I know but this secret is worth keeping."

"Is there someone else?"

"No baby, look I know that I hurt you in the past but that part of me is gone and I know I'm asking you a lot but I just need for you to trust me just this once."

"Okay but I if feel like something fishy is going on I'm going to turn into inspector gadget."

"(Laughing) and I wouldn't even blame you."

"So what time will you be back?"

"At seven tonight."

"Are you sure that there's no one else?"

"I promise you baby you're the only one for me."

"I love you," I said.

"I love you too," he replied.

Chapter 20

He got ready, kissed me good bye and then he left. I wanted so badly to follow him but I promised that I would trust him so instead of me following him I finished my breakfast and went to work. It wasn't that much to do because today was a slow day but I had to do as much as possible to make sure that I got all my hours. After I was done I gave my employees instructions and I told them who would close up for today and I left. Afterwards I met up with my girls. I wanted to tell them about Juelz strange ways but I didn't want their opinions because it could make me look at him differently and I really wanted to trust him. We made it to some condos and I didn't understand why they wanted to meet here.

"Hey ya'll," I greeted them.

"Hey girl," they greeted back.

"Why are we here?" I asked.

"That's the same thing that I would like to know," Kiera said.

"Well maybe I could help ya'll with that, you see Ace and I decided that we want to move in together," Terri said.

"But ya'll already live together in your apartment," I said.

"Yea but that's a one bedroom and he wants a bigger space so that we can start a family," Terri replied.

"Well that's nice and everything but I hope that he plans on putting a ring on it," Kiera said.

"Well actually he proposed to me last night," Terri said.

"Oh my god congratulations," I said.

"Thank you."

"So when is the wedding," I asked.

"Next spring," Terri replied.

"Awww I'm so happy for you I can't wait to help you plan your wedding, Kiera isn't this great news?" I asked.

"Yea, yea whatever."

"What's your problem?" Terri asked.

"Look I'm sorry it's just that Siy and I have been having problems," Kiera explained.

"What do you mean?" I asked.

"Lately he's been acting weird, he's been getting these strange phone calls and normally he wouldn't mind if I answered his phone but now he rushes to pick it up, the time that he leaves the house and come back are ridiculous, and I barely even get sex."

"So what are you saying?" Terri asked.

"I think that Siy is cheating on me," Kiera said.

"Come on Kiera you can't possibly think that I mean Siy is a good man," I said.

"Maybe he was but now he's changed," Kiera said.

"So what are you going to do?" Terri asked.

"I don't know I mean I love him and I really want to work it out but in order for us to get passed this he's going to have to come clean and change his ways," Kiera explained.

"And if he doesn't?" I asked.

"Then I have no choice but to leave," Kiera said.

"I'm so sorry and I hope everything works out," I said.

"Yea me too because honestly I like Siy and I just can't wrap my mind around him cheating on you," Terri said.

"Well anything is possible but I don't want this to spoil our day so what do we have planned?" Kiera asked.

"Well I was thinking that maybe we could go get our nails done and maybe tonight we can have a triple date at my house," I said.

"Ok but who's going to cook?" Terri asked.

"I don't know I'm not feeling up to this," Kiera said.

"Please do it for me and maybe I can pull Siy to the side and see what's really going on," I begged.

"Well ok but I can't promise you that we're going to be floating on clouds like everybody else," Kiera said.

"That's fine because I don't float I glide," Terri said laughing.

"Whatever you wish," Kiera responded.

"Okay now that everyone is happy can we go and look at some of these condos?" Terri asked.

"Yea but if you're not happy with these condos I mean you can always rent to buy mines since its paid off and I have to move all my stuff back into the house, it's a two bedroom, one and a half bath, a big living room, a nice size dining area, a big kitchen, two door garage, a big front and back yard, a nice size patio deck, a sunroom, and a big space down in the basement and you can turn it into whatever you want to turn it into and besides I'll only charge you 600 dollars a month it's 1,748 square feet if you pay it off the value has dropped so it would be $416,999.6 but like I said I can work with you."

"Well dang girl you sound like you should be in the real-estate business but that's sound like a good idea I mean these prices are outrageous and I really want this so I'll take it," Terri said.

"Okay well I'm off tomorrow and I got the movers coming out to get my things so maybe on Saturday you and Ace can come out and look at it, discuss it with each other, and then give me a call and let me know," I said.

"Okay I will but until then let's just look around these condos so that I can at least tell Ace that I tried and that I didn't like the prices," Terri said.

"Ok let's go," Keira said.

We went inside a couple of condos and I must admit that they were nice but the prices were a killer and some of them were just too small for the amount that they were asking for. I decided to keep looking and let Terri make her own decision. After walking through the condos we went and got our nails done. So far everything was going well and it was nice because I hadn't got my nails done with my girls in a while. We sat and talked like we hadn't talked in years and I really missed Star and although I knew that she would never come back the thought of all four of us being together again made me smile.

"What you over there smiling about?" Kiera asked.

"Nothing I was just thinking about if Star was here," I said.

"Me too look, I know that you guys said that it was no one's fault that Star was killed but I really feel responsible I mean sometimes I sit back and think about what our lives would have been like had I not stole those drugs and talked everyone into selling them. I was so Naïve and all I could think about was the fast money and that's the same thing that got one of my best friends killed and now because of me I will never get to see her get married, have children, or even grow old and even though I keep a smile on my face I think about that every day and I just thank you guys for forgiving me and not giving up on me," Terri said with tears welling up in her eyes.

"It was all of our faults if we had made a different decision none of us would be talking about Star as in past tense," Kiera said.

"Yea and besides this is what Star would have wanted she wouldn't have wanted to see us fighting like cats and dogs. Star was our strength she kept everyone together," I said.

We continued to talk and get our nails done and when we were finished I went to meet up with my mom and Mrs. Marie. When we finally met up we talked about the seating arrangements, the cake, the flower girl, and the food but I still couldn't find a dress but that would come at a later day because I had to make it home to cook. It was almost seven and I wanted to make it home before Juelz. So I got into my car and when I returned home I cooked dinner, took a shower, and I got ready for the night to begin. At seven thirty Juelz walked into the house.

"Hey Baby what's all this for?" he asked.

"We're having a triple date so I need for you to run upstairs, take a shower, and get ready," I said.

"Yes ma'am." He said being sarcastic.

At eight thirty there was a knock at the door. I went to open it.

"Hey ya'll come on in," I said greeting and hugging everyone.

"Hey," they all greeted back.

"Juelz will be down in a minute he's just getting dressed," I said.

"Tell him to get down here he ain't going to look no better than he looks every day," Siy said.

"That would be an insult if you didn't look like you just woke up out of your casket," Juelz said coming down the stairs.

"Oh that's cold, what's up man," Siy said to Juelz as they dapped each other down.

"Nothing much man I'm still surviving," Juelz said.

"I heard that." Siy said.

"I guess I didn't get an invitation to the club," Ace said.

"Come on man you know that you can't be left out," Juelz said.

"Yea and besides you the only one that came in your church attire," Siy said laughing.

"Well I'm sorry I thought that we were going on a date not going to bed," Ace replied laughing.

"How you been man?" Juelz asked Ace.

"Man just living day by day," Ace replied.

"Man I know that's right man so how is work life treating you?" Siy asked.

"Man it's stressful as always but when I get that check it's remarkable," Ace said.

"Yea man money is always guaranteed to make a man smile," Siy said.

"Exactly," Juelz agreed.

"Okay boys enough about jobs and money we're on a date so all eyes and attention will be on us tonight," I said.

"Baby I can keep my eyes on you all night," Juelz responded.

"Okay enough of the freaky talk this is dinner not dessert," Kiera said.

"Oh so you're going to be my dessert for tonight?" Siy asked.

"Not even if you were on your death bed," Kiera replied.

"What Kiera meant to say was not tonight but everyone just sit down so that we can start dinner, Siy can you come and help me in the kitchen?" I asked.

"I'll help you Ms Royal," Juelz said.

"No thank you I need Siy to help me," I replied.

"Ok no problem" Siy said as he followed me to the kitchen.

"So what do you need help with?" he asked.

"What's going on with you?" I asked.

"What do you mean?"

"Are you cheating on Kiera?"

"No I would never do that to her!"

"Then what's up with all these random calls and these weird times that you're leaving the house and coming back."

"Well I can't tell you right now."

"And why not?"

"Because it's not the right time."

"And you're positive that you're not cheating on her?"

"I'm 100% positive, wait is that what she thinks."

"Yes, I mean you don't give her a reason to think otherwise."

"Look I love Kiera with all my heart and I would never reach that level to hurt her like that, but I promise that it's nothing like that, listen do you think that you can keep her distracted so she won't start digging for things."

"I don't know I'm not trying to lose another best friend."

"I promise you that this won't affect your friendship at all just tell her that I told you what was going on and that you know for a fact that I'm not cheating."

"But I would be lying."

"But it would be for a good cause."

"I don't know."

"Please I don't want to lose her."

"Okay but if you are up to something dirty and I lose my friend you are going to lose your life."

"I would never put you in a situation like that just trust me."

"If I hear that one more time."

"I know but I'm begging you please."

"Alright, alright already, I'll talk to her."

"Thanks lil sis."

"Don't thank me just yet."

"Is everything ok in here?" Juelz asked peaking his head inside the kitchen door.

"Yea we good, we're bringing the food now," I said as we picked up the food and carried it out to the dinner table.

We bowed our heads, said our prayers, and then we dug into our meal. We talked amongst each other about politics, sports, and love. We left the dinner table played a few games and then we called it a night. After everyone was gone Juelz and I cleaned up the house, took a shower, and we fell asleep in each other arms. The next morning Juelz got up, got dressed, and left to go gods knows where.

I tried to keep my mind distracted so that I wouldn't start having negative thoughts so I began cooking myself breakfast when I was interrupted by a phone call.

"Hello."

"So did you find out why he's been creeping around?" Kiera asked.

"Yes I did," I lied.

"Ok and"

"And I can't tell you!"

"What do you mean you can't tell me?"

"I made him a promise."

"What do you mean you're my friend not his?"

"I know and I wouldn't hold anything back from you but this is important."

"Ok so can you at least tell me if he's cheating."

"We spoke and he's not cheating."

"Then what is he up to?"

"I can't tell you but trust me when I tell you that it's nothing bad and soon he's going to tell you everything but now is not the right time."

"I'm going to trust you and I'm going to back off but if I find out otherwise both of you are going to die."

"Okay I understand."

"So what are you doing today?"

"Well right now I'm cooking myself breakfast and I'm waiting for the movers to bring me my things so that I can go clean up the condo so that I can take Terri and Ace on a tour."

"And just how are you supposed to do all of that with a big belly?"

"Excuse me."

"I'm just saying big mama now that you're farther along there's things that you can no longer do like you use to do."

"For your information I am the first pregnant girl that's not being held back because of a big belly, I can still do everything that I use to do with the exception of sex. I mean really I can't stand to be around those pregnant handicap girls."

"What exactly is a pregnant handicap girl?"

"The girls that can't do anything for themselves it's always give me this, give me that, I can't do this, I can't do that, and it never gets old."

"Oh you're so mean."

"I'm not mean I'm just honest."

"Well I'm still coming over to help you so get over it."

"Really so you're turning me into a handicap pregnant girl."

"No I'm turning you into a friend that just happen to be a girl, pregnant, and handicap."

"Ugggh."

"You'll be okay big mama just give me a minute and don't move until I get there."

"Whatever."

"Yes I love you too," and she hung up

I finished cooking breakfast, I ate, took a warm bubble bath, watched the movers put my things in the places that I asked them to, and then I waited for Kiera. When she made it I was already, ready to leave.

"So you were going to leave without me although I asked you to wait for me?"

"No I was just going to wait on the porch."

"You are such a terrible liar."

"I know, so are you ready to go."

"Yea let's head out."

Chapter 21

We made it to the condo and we cleaned all the appliances from top to bottom, cleaned all the windows, mopped the floors, vacuumed the carpet upstairs and down stairs, mowed the lawn front and back, swept the garage and drive way and instead of me waiting for Saturday I decided to call Terri and Ace and we waited for them to arrive. When they finally made it we walked all through the condo and I could tell just from looking at their faces that they were excited.

"Okay we've looked around so we're going to go home and discuss it and I'll call you tomorrow," Terri said.

"Okay talk to you, tomorrow," I said.

After they left I thanked and hugged Kiera and then I made my way home I was so exhausted and I was very much in need of a warm bath and a full body massage. When I got out of the car I saw Juelz car parked and I knew that he was home. I opened the door and I saw rose pallets going all the way up the stairs. I followed the rose pallets and I came face to face with Juelz standing near the bathroom with a towel.

"Your bath water awaits you my Royal Queen."

I went into the bathroom and there were also rose pallets in the tub

"Oh baby this is so sweet."

"Only for my queen and when you are done bathing I will have a full body massage, fruits, and juice awaiting you."

"Awww baby I love you."

"I love you too, now come my queen and let me help you undress."

"Okay my king."

I proceeded to get in the tub I took me a nice, warm, bubble bath and after I was done Juelz gave me a massage that I would never forget. I wanted so badly for him to make love to me but that would have to wait until my body was normal again. I would normally go to sleep afterwards but instead I lied there and listen to Juelz breathing and I thought how far we had come. I couldn't believe that the man that deflowered me would be the man that I married I know that, that might had sounded crazy but growing up my mom always told me that my body was a Jewel and I had to be careful who I gave it to because the boys just wanted one thing and then they were on to the next girl and once you gave it away you couldn't get it back and I felt so good to know that not only was he the first man that ever touch my body but now we was also fighting towards him being the only man that touched my body. I guess I had to be deep into my thoughts because I caught myself smiling. I kissed the love of my life softly on the lips and I went to bed. The next morning, I woke up to breakfast in bed but this time instead of Juelz being in a rush to leave he lied in the bed in his pajamas.

"Good morning sleepy head," Juelz greeted me.

"Good morning, so you're not in a rush today?" I asked.

"No today is my resting day and I want to spend it with you."

"Awww baby that's nice and everything but I actually have plans with my mom and Portia."

"Really?"

"Yes but I can cancel if you would like."

"No don't do that you go and have fun."

"Are you sure?"

"Yea you go right ahead and maybe if the girls aren't with their father Portia won't mind me keeping them."

"Awww that's so sweet."

"Yea I love my nieces and I can also get a little practice in before my son comes"

"Well call her and see today just might be your lucky day."

He called Portia and she was okay with him keeping the girls. An hour later she dropped the girls off and we were on our way but not before I stopped by my mom house to pick her up. She walked outside to get inside the car and to say that my mom was beautiful was an understatement. I hoped that I would age gracefully just like my mom.

"Hey mama."

"Hey sweetie how, are you and the baby?"

"We're good so are you ready to go?"

"Let's head out"

We left and twenty minutes later we pulled up in front of the bridal shop

"Okay ladies let's find my dream wedding dress," I said.

"You're not going to turn into a bridezilla are you?" my mom asked.

"Really mama."

"Hey you know that you can go from an angel to two horns really quick."

"That is such an insult."

"That is the truth now let's go and find my dress I mean your dress."

We went inside and we were greeted very nicely by the workers.

"Welcome would you ladies like something to drink"

"I know we do but this one well as you can see she out of order," my mama said.

"I know that's right," Portia agreed.

"Well, excuse me ladies I'm not doing anything other than standing here," I responded.

"We sorry girl but we can't cut out our fun because you knocked up you should have told my brother to pull out" Portia said laughing.

"I couldn't it was too good," I said laughing.

"See what happens when a man gives you good sex you get pregnant and walk around like a big blimp for nine whole months," my mama said laughing.

"Corrections that's a big sexy blimp to you now let's find my dream wedding dress," I said.

We search for an hour but when I came across the perfect dress I just knew it was the one because it screamed my name and I couldn't resist it. It was the most beautiful dress that I had ever seen in my life it was a peachy color, it was sleeveless but it came down to hug my shoulders, it had a sash around the waist with rhinestones and it rested on my back as a big ribbon looking bow, it had a spilt on each side, and each split had ruffles around them. And to give an even better look I would buy shoes with the resemblances of Cinderella but with specks of peach in them. It was so nice and my mother was only able to say a few worlds.

"You look so beautiful!" my mom cried.

"Thank you mama,"

"Oh my god girl that dress is the one," Portia said.

"Thank you," I said. I tried on a few more dresses afterwards but I was for sure that that dress was the one. After I ordered my dress I left, dropped my mom back off, and I made my way home. Portia sat with us a little while longer and talked before her and the girls packed up and left. Afterwards I took me a nice warm bubble bath and then I cuddled with my future husband.

"How was your day Ms. Royal?"

"It was great everyone got along and I found my dream wedding dress."

"That's good news."

"Yea I know."

"So why are you looking so down?"

"Babe I just don't want to be fat and disgusting on my wedding day and honey moon."

"Ms. Royal you can never look fat and disgusting to me you the most beautiful woman that I have ever seen in my life pregnant or not nothing can change that."

"Aww baby that was sweet but I don't believe you."

"So what are you saying?"

"Maybe we can postpone the wedding until I have the baby because then that would be the perfect wedding day."

"Babe are you getting cold feet and making excuses so that you don't have to marry me."

"No that's not it at all I just want our wedding day to be something to remember."

"That would be a day to remember and besides if you wait until you have the baby you're going to have to first find a babysitter that don't mind keeping a small baby, then you've been talking about breast feeding so that means that you're going to have to pump enough milk to last until we come back, and we are supposed to be gone for two weeks and breast milk only last for three to five days without being frozen, and not to mention that you will be calling every thirty minutes because you will be a first time mother and you're not going to want to be away from our son."

"You may be right but I just don't want to walk down the aisle looking like a big house."

"Baby you won't be I promise."

"What are you going to do hold my stomach for me."

"I can either do that or I can put two big girls next to you that's guaranteed to make you look smaller."

"Ha, ha, ha."

"You know that was funny."

"It tickled me a little."

"I love you baby."

"I love you too."

I kissed Juelz goodnight and I went to bed. Two days had passed and everything was good and in order except for I still hadn't found my wedding cake so after work I was planning on meeting with both of my moms and go cake tasting. I kissed Juelz goodbye as he got ready to go to an anonymous destination and I left for work. I pulled up to work and as I was about to enter the building I noticed some commotion. I heard two different male voices demanding everybody to get on the ground so instead of me going inside I decided to turn around and call the cops but before I could do that I was distracted by a man with a gun against my temple.

"You better not press send bitch!"

"Ok please don't kill me I'm pregnant!"

"Well maybe if you do what I say you'll live now go inside the building."

I did just what I was told and I went inside.

"Are you the manager?"

"Yes."

"Well, manager I'm going to need for you to unlock the cash register."

"I can't I don't have my key!"

"And just where is your key?"

"It's in the back."

"Well let's go and get it, but don't try anything stupid because I won't hesitate to blow your brains all over these walls."

I did what he asked and I grabbed the key. We headed back to the front and I open the cash register so that he could get the money and just when I thought that everything was over with he flipped the script.

"Okay so now I'm going to need someone to go with us so that I can make sure that the cops don't follow us," he said.

"Take that bitch!" his companion said pointing at me.

"Hell naw that bitch useless I'm going to take her," he said pointing at Brittany a young, Hispanic eighteen-year-old girl that I had just hired a week ago.

"No please don't take her take me!" I said crying.

"Ain't nobody going to take you but Jesus if you don't lay face down on the ground now lay down!" He shouted while pointing the gun at my face. Knowing that there was really nothing else that I could do I lied face down on the ground looking helpless and sobbing as they drug Brittany to their car and drove away and when I was sure that they were gone I picked up my phone, shaking, and in shock and I called the police. After hanging up with them I called Juelz. When the police arrived I told them what happened and although I couldn't describe their faces because they wore masks I could describe their car. After answering all the cops' questions, I couldn't have been more excited to see Juelz face than I was now.

"Baby are you okay?" He asked

"Yes I just want to go home."

"Ok," he turned around and looked towards the door ."Siy I need you to drive my car home and I'm going to drive Royal's car."

"A'ight."

Chapter 22

Siy took Juelz keys and we left and when we finally made it home I just sat in one spot in shock. Later on that night when we got ready for bed I was too scared to close my eyes and every sound that I heard scared me. So instead of me going to bed I went down stairs and I called my girls. And when I had the both of them on the phone I just blurted it out.

"We got robbed today."

"What, Royal are you okay?" Kiera asked.

"Yea I'm good I'm just shook."

I explain everything that happened and how it went down.

"So what happened to Brittany?" Terri asked.

"I still don't know I'm just waiting by the phone hoping to hear some good news."

"That's a lot of stress to go through especially since you're pregnant," Kiera said.

"Yea Royal you need to get some rest and try to put your mind at ease," Terri said.

"How am I supposed to put my mind at ease when Brittany is out there going through god knows what and it's all my fault," I broke down crying.

"Royal it's not your fault you did everything that you could," Kiera said.

"You really did I mean what could you have possibly done knowing that if you didn't do what they said they would have killed you too and they would have still taken her and you have a child to think about," Terri said.

"But she's somebody's child too I just really wanted to help her."

"I know baby girl but it was just out of your hands," Kiera said.

"I know and that's the second time," I said crying and thinking about Star and how that ended. As I was breaking down I felt a hand touch my shoulder and it startled me.

"Baby come on it's time to go to bed," Juelz said.

"I'm not tired."

He grabbed my phone.

"Terri, Kiera I'm sorry but I think Royal needs to get some rest so I'll have her to call you in the morning," he said.

"Okay we understand go take care of our girl," they replied.

"I will," he said and then he hung up.

"Why did you do that?"

"Because the baby and I need you to get some rest."

"I can't sleep knowing that she's just out there!"

"And just what are you supposed to do by staying up and crying your eyes out."

"Are you mocking me?"

"No I would never do that but all I'm saying is that you have had a drastic day and a little rest won't hurt and if you don't do it for me do it for our son."

"Alright."

I went upstairs and I called it a night. The next morning, I called off of work, waited by the phone, and turned the TV on the news to see if I would hear some good news. While sitting in the living room waiting on the news my phone began to ring.

"Hello."

"Good morning how you feeling?" Kiera asked.

"I'm still freaking out!"

"So did you watch the news last night."

"No why do you ask?"

"Because they found Brittany."

"What, is she alright, where is she?"

"She's fine she was able to escape when they made a pit stop."

"Did they....you know?"

"They haven't said anything about it so I'm guessing not but she should be at home or somewhere safe with the family if you want to call her."

"I don't know I don't think that I can face her after that."

"Royal for the last time that was not your fault."

"Yea I hear you but I'm cleaning up around the house so let me call you back."

"Okay and I love you."

"I love you too."

I knew that I had lied but at this moment I no longer wished to discuss the situation I mean I could still see the helpless look on her face when they drug her away. While in deep thought Juelz came down dressed and ready to head out.

"Ok baby I'm on my way out."

"Okay I'll see you later."

"Are you going to be alright sitting here by yourself?"

"Yea."

"Are you sure because I can always make a few calls and stay here with you."

"No you go ahead and I'll call you if I need you."

"Ok I love you."

"I love you too."

He left and I decided to swallow my pride and contact Brittany. We spoke and she ensured me that everything was ok, nothing happened, and she didn't blame me for what took place but she did tell me that she would have to quit and after what had gone on I couldn't blame her because I had been thinking a lot and honestly I was too afraid to return back to work so I myself had a decision to make. Instead of me going to hang with anyone I decided to take a walk and sit in the park and think. When I finally made it I found the nearest bench and I watched the kids play on the playground and I couldn't do anything but smile and think about how my son would be. I thought about him waking me up in the mornings, me changing his diaper, me feeding him, him saying his first words, him crawling, him walking, and everything else that I had to look forward to. These past couple of days had been difficult but I was willing to dust myself off and keep it pushing and I would start with my work place. I loved my job and I was very blessed to get it but after all I had been through I had to think about the safety of me and my unborn son now don't get me wrong I would miss my coworkers and friends but at this moment I felt like god was pushing me to something better, something greater than what I had going on and you best to believe that I wasn't going to be afraid to find out just what that was. I sat at the park a little while before making the call and setting up a meeting with my boss I know that it would have just been easier to quit over the phone but I was professional before anything. I left the park, went home, watched a movie, and then I went to sleep but an hour later my nap was interrupted by a knock at the door. I went to answer the door.

"Hi mom."

"I just love to hear you call me that but you know why I came over here."

"Yea come on in and have a seat, you know Juelz is gone but if you don't have anything else to do we can go for lunch."

"Oh my god you forgot!"

"I forgot what?"

"You, your mother, and I are supposed to go cake tasting."

"Oh my god I totally forgot, let me just go upstairs, get dressed, and tell my mama to meet us there!"

"Ok."

I ran upstairs, got ready, and I called my mom on my way out the door. My mom didn't answer but when we arrived she was already there.

"Hey mama I been calling you," I said hugging her.

"I know but I wanted to surprise you."

"So are you ladies ready to taste some cake," I asked.

"Yes we are," they said.

We went inside and not only did the cakes smell good they looked good too. We sat down and the baker brought us the first sample.

"The first one is a white almond wedding cake"

We all took a bite of our sample and it was good but it wasn't what I was looking for

"This is okay but it's not exactly what I'm looking for"

"Would you like to try the next sample" he asked

"Yes please" I responded

The second was a lemon raspberry cake, it was very moist, it was soft, and it was sweet, but it just had too many flavors going on for me so we asked for the next one.

The third one was a tropical Caribbean cake and it was very delicious and I wasn't the only one that like it, Mrs. Marie seemed to like it very much herself but I had to keep my options open so I decided to taste one more cake. The fourth cake was a hazel nut delight and it was very delicious and although my mother loved the cake I was leaning towards the tropical Caribbean cake.

"Okay ladies now let's make a vote."

"Okay," they said.

"Well since I'm going to be the bride I 'll choose first and I choose the tropical Caribbean cake," I said.

"And I second that vote," Mrs. Marie said.

"Well I vote The fourth cake hazel nut delight," my mom said.

"All votes are in and mama we out voted you."

"It wouldn't be the first time," my mom said.

"What is that supposed to mean?" I asked.

"Since Juelz proposed to you Marie has been the one that you asked to do things when it comes to planning the wedding you never once asked my opinion on anything not even your wedding dress you just took me along for the ride but I had no say so on anything and now she gets to choose the cake too."

"Mama it's not like that."

"Yes, it is you're trying to let her take my place, look I get that I didn't like Juelz at first because of the way that he made his money but since then I have stepped back and let you live your life but you don't have to cross me out completely."

"Mama that's not what I'm doing."

"Paris I'm not trying to steal your daughter, come on now I have a daughter and I wouldn't want anyone to do that to me."

"Well you go marry your daughter off and leave me and mine alone."

"Whoa, whoa, whoa, this have gone far enough, I apologize Mrs. Marie but can you please excuse us?" I asked.

"Yea sure no problem," Mrs. Marie replied.

I grabbed my mom by the arm and I pulled her to the side.

"Now can you explain to me where all of this is coming from and why you just attacked Mrs. Marie for no reason at all?"

"I'm sorry I just feel like I'm losing you, I mean you're my only child and since the engagement I barely see you or get any calls from you and to see how Close You and Marie are it hurts my feelings and it makes me feel like you're closing me out."

"Mama that's not the case at all, you are a very busy woman and I just didn't want to be selfish and put too much stress on you all on the account of my wedding. If you would have pulled me to the side and said hey I want more to do I would have had no problem giving you more."

"I just don't want to lose you."

"Mama you can never lose me I'm always going to be your baby girl until the day that you or I take our last breath."

"I love you."

"I love you too mama."

"I guess I owe someone an apology."

"I guess you do."

We went back over to where Mrs. Marie was.

"Marie I would like to apologize for the way that I acted and treated you I was over reacting and I was wrong."

"I accept your apology and I would like to thank you for you making things right, getting to know you have been great and I would never want you to feel like you're being crossed out so the next time you feel that way just let me know so I can back off."

"You don't have to back off I was just being selfish, and besides Royal is a great young woman and she deserves all the love that she gets."

"Aww mama that was so sweet, so now that we're back on track how about we all go out for drinks."

"No you're pregnant so how about you go home and get some rest and Paris and I go out for some drinks," Mrs. Marie said.

"I know that's right girl," my mama said.

"Now whose being scratched out?" I asked.

"No hard feelings it's just life but as soon as you drop that baby we'll be the first one to take you out for drinks but for now we'll see you later and we love you," Mama said as they both hugged me and left.

"Oh no they didn't," I said as I got into my car and drove home. When I made it home I had nothing to do so I decided to call my girls but they were at work or school so there I was again alone but I had one more person that I could depend on.

"Hello."

"Hey Portia are you busy?"

"No I'm just sitting here by myself looking crazy, the girls are with their father and Chase is at work."

"Well I'm in the same boat with the exception of the kids so what do you say you come over and we can watch movies together."

"That sounds nice but I will be bringing some wine."

"Oh lord don't do me like that."

"Oh don't worry you can have a glass or two I asked my doctor and they said that it would be fine."

"Ok well cool then bring the wine"

"I'll be there in a half hour."

"Okay girl see you soon."

I got up and went to the kitchen and I decided to whip up a dish. I put on some bake fish, bake potatoes, and I made a salad. While I was in the kitchen checking the food I heard the doorbell ring. When I peeped out of the glass it was Portia.

"Girl come on in don't just stand out there looking crazy."

"Oh girl it smells good in here what are you cooking."

"Something simple."

"Something simple like what."

"Bake fish, bake potatoes, and a salad."

"Well that will go great with this red wine."

"Yes it will but first let me put it in the freezer so that it can get chilled."

"Ok."

I went inside the kitchen and I placed the wine in the freezer.

"So what will we be watching today," Portia asked.

"Well since you're the guest it's your pick."

"Girl you know that I love a good throwback movie so we are going to watch Waiting To Exhale."

"Girl that's one of my favorite movies."

"I know honey I watched that movie so much that I could have been one of the characters in it."

"Girl you and me both because that movie shows just because you go through something you don't have to stay stuck in that situation."

"I know that's right girl and I have been through some messed up situations, you know when I met the triplets daddy he didn't reveal to me that he was married until I told him that I was pregnant and then he wanted to claim his wife talking about he had to do what was best for her and that was to cut all ties with me and I'm like well where was your wife when you sleeping with me only to find out later that she knew nothing about us and he was really getting rid of me so that he can save his own ass five years together and never not even once did he mention his wife."

"Yea well if you think that that's something try being with a man that forgot to tell you that oh baby by the way I do coke and I'm a swinger."

"Oh my, that's a lot."

"Yea just think about how much it was when I caught them in action."

"Girl I would have chopped his dick off!"

"Girl please I was too busy trying to get out of there and save my virginity to even think about it," I said laughing

"I know that's right I would have run so fast smoke would have been left behind."

"If it wasn't in reality it most definitely was in my head."

"And then you found my brother."

"Your brother was the one that offer me a ride that night he really saved my life."

"Now that's a real love story maybe you need to make a movie out of your life."

"Girl I wish, oh excuse me for a minute."

I went inside the kitchen and pulled the food out the oven and when I was sure that it was done I served the plates with wine. We watched Waiting To Exhale and after we were done we turned on some old school jams and we danced. We had so much fun that we couldn't do anything but laugh.

"Girl you like the sister that I never had," Portia said.

"Girl the same here I mean don't get me wrong I love my girls we been tight since pre k and I also consider them my sisters but you just remind me so much of my friend Star."

"Oh I heard about her that was some of the saddest news that I have heard."

"Yea me too but I know that's she's looking down and watching over me."

"Your own personal guardian angel."

"Yep."

We talked a little more before our fun was interrupted by Juelz.

"Hey sis."

"Hey big bro."

"What ya'll doing in here."

"Talking," I said.

"Royal I know you ain't drinking no wine" Juelz said.

"It's okay bae I only had one glass and the doctor said that it was fine."

"Portia you in here helping to get your nephew drunk."

"He will not be drunk it's just one glass so stop over reacting, now how was your day."

"It was good but I already know how ya'll day was so I'm not even going to attempt to ask."

"That's good because we weren't going to tell you anyway" Portia said laughing.

"Whatever big head" Juelz said

"Well I had fun hanging out with you today Royal but I have to go now my man will be home soon," Portia said.

"I had fun with you too, call me when you get home and drop by sometimes."

"Ok I will and if you ever get bored you are free to stop by."

"Okay girl see you later."

"Alright."

Portia got in her car and left.

"That was nice to see my sister and my soon to be wife getting alone," Juelz said.

"Yea I had fun."

"So what did you do"

"Well first me and my mom's went cake tasting and there was a bump in the road but everything was straightened out, then I stopped by the park to get some fresh air, and then I invited Portia and you know the rest, so how was your day."

"It was good."

"So are you ready to tell me where you head off to almost every day?"

"It's not time."

"Okay but don't come back here with no children or side chicks."

"I won't I promise," He said kissing me.

"Okay are you ready to eat."

"I'm starving."

"Well sit down and relax and I'll be back with your food."

I had no problem with catering to my man I mean after all the times he had catered to me tonight would be his night and he most definitely would enjoy it. I went into the kitchen, fixed him a plate, fixed him a glass of wine, and I served him like the king that he is. While he was eating his food I decided to give him a massage.

"Mmmm baby that feels good."

"Of course it does I got the magic fingers."

"I can tell because this food is delicious."

"Thank you baby," we kissed each other so passionately, I was most definitely in love with this man. I left his side and I decided to go upstairs and run his bath water. I turned off all of the lights and I lit and put candles all around the tub. When I was done I went down stairs, cleared the table, and then I lead my man to the bathroom.

"So my queen ran my bath water that's sweet baby."

"Only for my king."

"Are you trying to spoil me."

"You spoil me so we should be able to spoil each other."

"You want to get in with me."

"Baby if you would have asked me that seven months ago I wouldn't have had any problems but now there would be no space for the both of us but thank you for asking."

"Come on baby you can sit on daddy's lap."

"I don't want to hurt the baby."

"Come on I promise to go slow."

"I can't I'll crush you but if you really want to try it I would like to be comfortable."

"Okay what makes you comfortable."

"Lying on my side."

"Okay then let's go."

"Oh no Mr. Man we have to get cleaned up first, so I'm going to hop into the shower, you enjoy your bath and I'll see you when you get out."

Chapter 23

I went and I got into the shower. I was very anxious because I hadn't made love to my fiancé in a while because I didn't want to hurt the baby but I did miss the feel of him and the passionate love that we made. I knew that it would be different because of my situation but we would most definitely take it slow. After taking my shower I lied naked in the bed and I waited for Juelz to get out of the tub. Twenty minutes later he came out the bathroom dripping wet with nothing to hide the gift that he was given. I just lied there and watched him as he walked towards me with his glistering body.

"Baby you are so beautiful."

"Thanks sexy but instead of you talking about it you need to get over here and show me just how sexy I am."

"You don't have to ask me twice."

I knew that I couldn't lay on my back so I decided to get on all fours. He came up behind me and he began kissing on my neck, I moaned and shivered a little as the chills ran down my spine. He began kissing on my back as he entered me very slowly. It felt so good that I lost my breath. We moved slow until we caught a rhythm. Slowly he rolled me onto my side, he nibbled on my ear and neck, and he whispered sweet nothings in my ear. I rolled him on to his back and I got on top with my back towards him he kissed on the nape of my neck on down to my spine. I thrusted up and down on his man hood until my walls couldn't take it and it released, but we weren't done just yet. He picked me up and carried me around the room taking me up and down his man hood as we continued to make passionate love all night. The next morning, I got up to start my day but this was different, instead of waking up to my normal breakfast in bed I woke up to a small card that sat on my pillow and it read:

Dear Royal

My sweet, sweet queen since I first lied my eyes on you I knew that you were the one and I knew that you would be mine. It took a little while but at the end it was all worth it. Although we had a rough patch we made it through and I just want to say thank you for giving me a second chance so to show my appreciation I have ran you a nice bubble bath, I bought you a beautiful dress it is lying at the bottom of the bed, I cooked you breakfast, there's a hair dresser waiting down stairs and when you are done the limo will be outside waiting. Please don't ask any questions I really want to surprise you.

Love always

Juelz

Chapter 24

I lied in the bed smiling because my man was doing everything in his power to show me that he loved me. Although I didn't fall in love with him for his material things I did fall in love with him because of his personality, he's intelligent, his commitment, his big heart, the way he makes me smile, laugh, and everything else that made him, him. I didn't know how long we would be together but those were the things that I never wanted him to change. This relationship was a part of me and I was in it for the long run. I got up, went to eat breakfast took my bath, put on my silver dress. The neck came down to rest upon my breast and showed some cleavage, around the waist was a nice black belt, and the bottom of it was loose and it fell to my knees. I slid my foot inside of my four inch, black, red bottom heels. I went down stairs and got my hair done. It was a side part on the left and it was wand all over. After I was done getting my hair done I went upstairs, did my make up and put on my plum lip stick. I made it outside and there was a limo outside waiting. We greeted each other, he told me his name, opened my door, and I got inside. I wanted to ask so many questions but I decided against it. We drove for a while. Finally, we pulled up in front of The Ultimate Lobster Bar. The driver came around and opened my door. I got out of the car and I entered the building. They greeted me and showed me to my table. When I made it to my table I saw my man standing there with a nice black suit on holding a dozen roses in his hands.

"Good afternoon my beautiful lady."

"Good afternoon sexy."

"These are for you" He said passing me the roses.

"Oh thank you."

"Have a seat," he said as he pulled my chair out.

"Thank you, you are such a gentleman," I said as I sat down.

The waitress came over, introduced herself, gave us a menu, and she offered us something to drink.

"I will have a water," I said.

"I will also like a water," Juelz said

"Ok I will be right back with your water and to take your order?" she said.

"Thank you" Juelz said

She walked off and left the table.

"So you're drinking water now?" I asked.

"Of course I didn't want to tempt you I mean after all this day is all about you."

"Baby that's sweet but why is the day all about me."

"Because I really love you and you're very much worth it. Look if someone would have told me almost a year ago that I would be with you I wouldn't have believed them and when I say that I don't mean it lightly. I mean I knew that I wanted you from the first time I lied eyes on you and I knew that it would be a challenge getting your attention and when I finally got it and you gave me that chance I was scared that I would mess everything up I mean I kind of sort of did but I fixed it and now that I have you back I don't ever want to lose you again and in order for me to prove this to you I have to show it and I most definitely don't mind telling the world that you're my woman. I know a lot of men have said it but I truly believe that I'm the luckiest man on earth. Baby I love you and as long god allows me to breathe this air and live on this green earth I will make sure that you always know that and that you're always happy."

"Aww baby I love you too, that's so sweet you're going to make me cry."

"No you can't cry just yet you got to save those tears for the wedding."

"Oh you want me to look like an emotional wreck at my wedding," I said laughing.

"No baby not at all but you know once daddy get in his feelings and I let everything out you're not going to be able to control your emotions."

"True but I won't be by myself."

"You most definitely won't."

In the middle of our conversation the waitress came back to the table with our water and to take our order.

"I'll have the broiled chopped sirloin steak," I said.

"I'll have the dino's pan roasted chicken vesuvio," Juelz said.

"Will that be all for you?" the waitress asked.

"Yes thank you," Juelz said.

"So how are the wedding plans going since you completely kicked me out?" Juelz asked.

"Oh baby I'm sorry."

"Don't be sorry I just want you to be happy I was only being sarcastic."

"Well it's going great with the exception of the location but we can find that together."

"So what would you like the location to be like."

"I'm not quite sure yet all I know is that I want it to be outside."

"Don't worry we got time."

"No baby we only have a couple of weeks and I don't want to get stuck having a wedding just anywhere."

"Don't worry baby we are going to find something before time is up."

"Oh my god I'm turning into a bridezilla!"

"No you're not you're just nervous and want everything to go well and that's normal."

"I like how you tried to make everything positive but honestly baby I think that I'm a bridezilla."

"Just a little but like I said there's nothing wrong with wanting everything to be perfect.

"So how is everything going with you?"

"Everything is going just as expected and before you get nervous and start worrying baby I just want you to know that soon I'm going to put your mind at ease and if you can just give me until our wedding day to tell you everything that will mean a lot to me and I know what I'm asking you to do is a lot for you but baby trust me when I tell you that it will all be worth it at the end."

"You're not going to rip my heart out and stomp all on it are you?"

"Baby I would never do that I worked to get you in my life and I don't intend on losing you we're in this together until the good lord calls me home."

"That's right because you belong to me."

"And you already know that you're mines forever."

He kissed me over the table. About twenty minutes later the waitress brought our food to the table. We ate, talked, laughed, and we left. The night ended well. A week had passed and I had finally found a place to have our wedding. I wanted an outside wedding so it would be by a beautiful lake. I was so excited I had already told them about the decorations and the flowers that I wanted and now that I had most of all the wedding stuff I was going to stop by my mom's house and give her the job of sending out all of the invitations. I pulled up to her house and I could see Ronald's car parked outside. I got out of the car and knocked on the door.

"Hey baby," my mama said hugging me.

"Hey mama what you doing?"

"Nothing just keeping myself busy watching tv since I'm off work today."

"Well speaking of being off of work today I got a favor I need to ask you."

"Go ahead run it across me."

"I just wanted to know if you would do me the honor of sending out the invitations for the wedding?"

"I would love to. Do you have them with you?"

"That's the thing you said you never had a say so with the wedding so I'm letting you go get them you can design them however you want."

"Oh my god I'm so excited!"

"So here's the money and if you need me for anything you know my number."

"Yea, yea, yea now get out so I can get ready to go."

"Oh so you just going to throw me and your grand baby out like that?"

"I'm not throwing him out just you."

"You throwing him out to because he's in my tummy."

"Well he'll understand when he gets older now come on now I got to go."

"Wait mama I have one more thing to ask you."

"What is it?"

"Would you mind going out with me tomorrow to pick out the bride maid dresses with me? This time it's just going to be you and I and I promise to let you have your input."

"Yes I will I'm so excited!"

"Okay mama I love you."

"I love you too and I'll talk to you later."

I got in my car and I called my girls and asked them to meet up with me because we hadn't seen each other in a while. We all decided that today we would meet up at Terri's place and that's where I was on my way to. Finally, after driving over forty-five minutes I pulled up at Terri's place and as I got out the car I could see Kiera just pulling up behind me. When she got out of the car we greeted each other.

"Hey girl long time no see," Kiera said hugging me.

"Hey girl and I know I just been a little busy with the wedding plans."

"I know I understand you don't even have to explain but I can't wait to see my girl walk down that aisle and I get to be a part of it all."

"Of course you one of my best friends now let's go in here and check on this heifer."

"Let's go."

We walked to the door and rang the doorbell and when the door swung open she was more than happy to see us.

"My girls I'm so glad that ya'll are here come on in we got to catch up."

We went inside and she showed us to the living room.

"Have a seat would ya'll like anything to drink?" Terri asked.

"I just want some water," I said.

"Well bring me a glass of wine," Kiera said.

Terri left and returned with our drinks.

"This place looks good girl," I said.

"Thank you we tried to make it our own," Terri said.

"Well you definitely did that this place looks a whole lot different than when Royal lived here," Kiera said.

"It sure do, so he decorated it right, because I already know it wasn't you?" I asked.

"Well, Ms. Thang you would be wrong because I decorated this thing from top to bottom," Terri responded.

"Well, excuse me," I said laughing.

"You excused now pick your jaw up," Terri said laughing.

"So besides working and decorating the house what have you been up to?" Kiera asked Terri.

"Well I've been looking for wedding dresses and colors," Terri responded.

"I'm so happy for you, you deserve it," I said.

"Thank you, I'm happy for you too and we all deserve it," Terri said.

"Girl well I have yet to get mines," Kiera said.

"Well you won't be waiting for too long because Siy ain't letting you go nowhere," I said.

"Girl please if another man was to come and scoop me up now he probably won't even notice and even if he did he probably wouldn't even care," Kiera responded.

"Kiera stop it you know that Siy loves you," I said.

"And I believe that one hundred percent but does love really keep men around these days?"

"Hell yea," Terri and I said.

"You better check out our fingers," I said while we both flashed our ring finger.

"Look girl you just stressing over something small and making it into something big I'm starting to think that maybe you're trying to self-sabotage your own relationship," Terri said.

"I might be but why sit around living on cloud nine when the whole time your man can be making plans to ran away, leave, and go to paradise with another woman behind your back?" Kiera asked.

"First off you know that Siy is not like that and even if he was and you felt that way why would you even waste your time sticking with this man and this relationship until he gets tired and kick you to the curb," I said.

"So what you saying is that you think I need to leave him?" she asked.

"No what I'm saying is that deep down in your heart you know that you have a good man you're just frustrated and you don't know what else to do so you trying to find any way out of this relationship with a lie that makes you feel good with your decision," I said.

"Shut up Royal," Kiera said.

"You know that I'm right," I said.

"Okay maybe but before he was sneaking around and everything we had a perfect relationship."

"Exactly and with this man doing everything in his power to make you happy and he's giving you no reason not to trust him and this is his first time that he's asking you to trust him then you should have no problem doing just that I mean I love my man with all my heart but he has given me a reason not to trust him and I really want to but it's hard but Siy only have eyes for you I know because I see the way that he looks at you and how he smiles when he talks about you. Girl you better keep that good man because if you don't it will be a lot of lonely woman out there willing to snatch him up and do anything they got to do to keep him happy and around," I said.

"Preach sister!" Terri screamed.

"You right but I still want you to shut up," Kiera said laughing.

"So now that you're getting closer to the special day how are you feeling?" Terri asked me.

"Which special day?" I asked.

"Girl I wasn't even thinking about that but that's a good question. How are you feeling about both of them?" she asked.

"I feel ready, I mean you can never be fully prepared but I'm ready for anything that comes my way," I said.

"I want to be just like you when I grow up," Kiera said.

"Me too," Terri said.

"You girls are silly," I said.

"No for real since I've known you and I've known you for a long time you always knew what you wanted and you always knew just how to get it regardless of the consequences and how things turned out you went for it," Kiera said.

"Well that can be good and bad," I said.

"Well for you it's nothing but good things," Kiera said.

"Girl I surely hope so."

"Do ya'll realize that we haven't done this in a while?" Kiera asked.

"Of course how can I forget I mean I sit back and I think about all the times that we snuck out of our parents' house to go to parties," Terri said.

"Yep and then we grew up and we got into relationships," I said.

"Especially you girl you ditched us once you got with Juelz," Terri said laughing.

"Girl don't do that I checked up on ya'll," I responded.

"Yea when you weren't on your back," Kiera said as her and Terri laughed.

"Girl don't do me I wasn't always on my back," I said laughing.

"Well how did this happen?" Terri asked pointing at my fully grown belly.

"And don't say that you were raped because we all know that you gave that thing up willingly," Kiera said.

"I was drunk," I said.

"Really?" Terri asked.

"What? She said don't say that I was raped so my next excuse is that I was drunk," I said laughing.

"Ok don't let me catch you on Maury show," Terri said.

"Only if he denies him," I responded.

"Well I'm glad to say that he's a good man just like I said when you were giving him the side eye," Kiera said.

"Girl I had to because he was a pretty boy with a bunch of groupies," I said.

"And now?" Terri asked.

"And now he's a pretty boy with one groupie," I said laughing.

"Would you happen to be that groupie?" Kiera asked.

"I'm his groupie, his lover, his friend, and his number one fan," I said.

"Girl I heard that," Terri said.

Chapter 25

I stayed and had dinner with my friends. We had so much fun and I didn't want it to end but I knew that eventually it had to. We stayed up until one o'clock talking about everything up under the sun and when I made it home my man was lying on the sofa sleep as if he was waiting up for me. I didn't want to be rude so I woke him up with a kiss on the lip.

"Ms. Royal."

"How did you know?"

"Because you the only one better be kissing me like that and besides my mama you the only one better have that key."

"And you know it, now come on let's go upstairs."

A week had past and I was a week away from getting married. I was so excited but I was also nervous but nothing could change my mind when it came to me marrying the love of my life. I was in such a great mood because my mom had sent me a picture of my wedding invitations and they were so beautiful but today we were going to find the brides maid dresses. We had already looked at a few but they weren't what I was looking for but today I was determined to find them and I couldn't stop until I did because my wedding was right around the corner. After getting out the shower, getting dressed, and doing my hair I made it my business to do my makeup, have a toast and egg for breakfast and then I was on my way out of the door but as I opened it there stood a man about 5'9, caramel brown, nice body build, a fade, a nice smile, and he looked to be in his early forties.

"May I help you?" I asked.

"Royal?" he asked.

"Yes," I said suspiciously still trying to figure out exactly who this man was standing in my door way.

"It's me Donald, your father"

I had to take a step back because I just knew that this man hadn't just said that he was my father.

"What do you mean that you're my father?"

"I'm your biological father."

"How did you find out where I lived?" I asked.

"I did a little asking around and I bumped into someone that knew you and he told me where you lived."

"And who is that someone?"

"Your fiancé Juelz, look can I come in so that we can talk."

"No I don't think that I'm in that kind of space right now."

"Ok that's understandable so listen I'm going to give you time to think. This is my number I just moved back here so if at any time you want to talk i'm only one call away."

"Yea ok."

I waited until he walked away and I closed the door. My good day had quickly turned into a bad day I couldn't believe that Juelz had spoken to my dad and told him my location without speaking to me first. I was so furious and I would make sure that Juelz knew it when he got home but for now I still had to meet up with my mom for the bride maid's dresses. I looked out the window to make sure that the coast was clear. When I was sure that he was gone I hopped in my car and I went to meet up with my mom. When I made it to the bridal shop my mom was already waiting there for me.

"Hey baby girl."

"Hey mama"

"What's wrong?"

"Nothing we can talk about it later?"

"Are you sure?"

"Yea I'm sure let's go in here and find these dresses."

We went inside of the building in although I wanted to be into it so bad my mind was still weighing heavy on the fact that my dad had never even given me a chance out of the eighteen years that I had been on this earth and then all of a sudden he had woken up and decided that he wanted to be a part of my life. I had so much to say to him and I just wasn't sure how it would come out. So for now it was best if that man stayed away from me. I had to get my thoughts together so I could look at these dresses. The designer had already showed us a few but from me being deep into my thoughts I couldn't even describe what they looked like. I was finally brought out of my trance when the designer asked me

"Would you like to see some more dresses because we have some more in the back and I've noticed that none of these dresses have moved you?"

"Yes that will be fine," I said.

She went into the back and she brought back a line of dresses. I went through most of the dresses but nothing had caught my eye until I got to the back. It had one sleeve on the right, no sleeve on the left, it was a peachy color, it had a white ribbon around the waist, it fell very loosely to the feet, and a split rested on the right thigh. I was so excited and just as I were about to ask my mom's opinion she spoke

"Oh my god that is a beautiful dress you have to choose that one!" she said excitingly.

"You really think so?" I asked.

"Yes I do; this is going to be a beautiful wedding. I'm so happy for you baby."

"Awww thank you mama," I said hugging her.

"You welcome baby"

"Ok so this is going to be my bride maid's dresses I'm so excited."

After purchasing the dresses my mom decided that she wanted to go somewhere to eat. When we made it to the restaurant we found ourselves a table. I didn't want to bother my mama with all the extra things and mess up her day by talking about what had taken place so I decided to keep it to myself. As if she could read my mind or see through my soul or maybe it was just the worried expression that showed on my face that had given me away but she had to know.

"Sweetie what's wrong? You have been out of it all day and don't say nothing because I know when something is wrong with my child so what's eating at you?"

"Donald stopped by my house."

"Donald who? because you can't possibly be talking about the Donald that I know."

"If your baby daddy is the only Donald that you know well then I'm talking about him."

"First off how did he find out where you lived and what did he want?"

"He said that he bumped into Juelz and he told him and he claimed that he wanted to get to know me but really mama I'm not interested."

"Listen I don't want to be the reason that you make that decision by putting a lot of bitter things into your mind so; I say you should think about it and make your own decision and do just what's in your heart"

"But what could we possibly have to talk about he made up his mind about me the day that you said that you were pregnant so why should I care what he has to say."

"Well maybe you need to tell him how you truly feel, but who knows anyone can change and I don't want to be the reason that you don't ever have a father figure in your life, or your son has no grandfather I'm just saying maybe you should really consider hearing what he has to say."

"I don't know."

My mom and I finished lunch and then we parted ways. On my way back home I had a lot on my mind I kept trying to push it aside but it just kept coming back. I was so confused as to what I wanted to do because I really didn't know if I should hear him out. Forty minutes into driving I finally made it home. I was trying my best not to be stressed out and especially not at a time like this with my wedding coming up and a baby on the way. I tried to find things to do around the house to keep myself busy but I was very unsuccessful it got to the point where I was just so drained and I dozed off. I was awakened hours later by a kiss on the lips.

"Hi baby how was your day?"

"It's very interesting that you would be the one to ask that question."

"What is that supposed to mean?"

"Have you talked to anyone lately that I should know about?"

"No not that I know of."

"Oh really?"

"Yea really."

"So what about Donald?"

"Oh your dad."

"No my donor."

"Look it was nothing like that I was on my way to shoot some hoops with Siy and he pulled up on me. He said that he'd hired a private investigator to find his daughter because he hadn't seen her in a while. He gave me your name and everything and I told him that you were my fiancé. He said that he wanted to surprise you and that you would be happy to see him so I gave him the address."

"How could you be so irresponsible to give away my information like that ?You don't know if he was lying, a murderer, a rapist, or anything you just gave out my information."

"I wasn't being irresponsible I knew he wasn't lying because you look just like him and I just wanted to surprise you."

"Well that you did and not in a good way."

"Why are you acting like that? I did this for you, I mean what could he have done that was so bad."

"How about ditching the mother of his child while she was pregnant never once reaching out after her giving birth and now eighteen years later you decide to show up."

"I'm sorry I didn't know."

"And you never asked either."

"What do you mean I never asked I told you everything about me and it would've only been right if you had done the same thing."

"Don't try to flip this around on me this happened because you poked your nose around in someone else's business this had nothing to do with you and you had no right to do what you did."

"So this is what I get for trying to do something nice for you?"

"Oh is that what you call it well the next time that you want to do something nice for me buy me a dog."

"Wow well now that you got your true feelings out of the way I'm out."

"What do you mean you out?"

"Just what I said."

"You not going anywhere," I said grabbing his arm.

"I'm out," he said once again as he broke free of my grip.

"Well I won't be here when you get back."

He paused for a moment like if he was thinking about something before he grabbed the door knob and left. I was so angry and hurt at the same time. How could he try to turn this all around on me when clearly all of this was his fault. I tried calling his phone but my calls went unanswered. I tried texting but again no response. I sat up hours waiting to hear his key in the lock but it never came. I could just imagine what he was out there doing with all of those loose women and it hurt just thinking about it. I called my mom and although I tried my best not to cry I couldn't hold it in.

"Mama he left me."

"Honey calm down."

"I can't he just walked out on me, he could be out there with other women doing god knows what. He won't answer my calls or respond to my text and he haven't even come home."

"Sweet heart calm down; Juelz is down stairs sleeping on the couch; look he told me what took place and how you treated him and that was very wrong."

"So now you're on his side?"

"I'm not on anyone's side; look I get why you were upset about him telling a stranger your business but you could have gone about it in a different way."

"What was I supposed to do grab his hand and talk to him like he's three; mama he's a grown man, he's about to be a father and it's only right that he starts acting and thinking like an adult."

"You may be right but he met well look how would you feel if every time you made a mistake instead of someone letting you know how they felt about something they just jump down your throat."

"Mama I didn't jump down his throat."

"He told me the conversation that ya'll had and you actually did; look I'm not saying how you felt was wrong but how you did was totally disrespectful and I think that you owe him an apology."

"Maybe you're right; so can you send him back home."

"Not right now he just needs time to cool off but he'll be back in the morning."

"Okay mama."

"I love you."

"I love you too mama."

I hung up the phone with my mama and I was kind of upset that she would let him sleep on her couch instead of making him come back home but I was relieved to know that he wasn't out clubbing with all those loose women. I tossed and turned all night. The next morning when I woke up I didn't want to move out of bed but I knew that I couldn't mope around all day. I went down stairs and I began pulling food out of the refrigerator to cook breakfast but then I heard the noise that I had be anticipating on hearing the whole night it was Juelz key twisting inside of the lock. I was so excited but I couldn't show it on my face. Once he was inside the house he came straight into the kitchen.

"We need to talk," we both said at the same time.

"I'll go first," I said.

"No I will, look I know that I was hard on you last night and I realize what you were trying to do and although I didn't tell you what my and my dad's relationship was I would really appreciate it if next time you're in a situation like that you call me first but overall I just want to apologize."

"Listen I know why you were upset and that was a very immature move that I made considering that I grew up in the streets so I should have known better so I'm sorry and it will never happen again."

"Did you have breakfast?"

"No I left as soon as I woke up."

"Would you like breakfast?"

"I would love some but I got to go."

"But you just got here."

"I know so the only thing that I have time for is a shower."

"So what do you expect for me to do?"

"Maybe you can hang with your girls today but when I get back I promise that I will make it up to you."

"And you're sure that there's no one else."

"Baby you're the only one for me."

"You promise?"

"I put that on my life."

I continued cooking breakfast while he went upstairs to get ready. After he was done he left. I sat in front of the television eating breakfast I could have easily called my girls to hang but I just didn't have the energy to give. Afterwards I went to take me a soothing bath to ease my mind and when I was done I knew what it was that I had to do. I picked up the phone and I called an hour later the doorbell rang.

"I'm glad you called me thank you for giving me a chance."

"Don't thank me just yet."

I stepped back away from the door so that he could come inside. Afterwards I closed the door and I showed him to the living room.

"Nice place," he said.

"Thank you; now Donald now that we're face to face can you explain to me what would possess you to leave my mother while she was pregnant, come tracking my fiancé down, and come running back here to me eighteen years later like we would hold hands and run into the sunset together."

"I know that you might be a little upset."

"That's an understatement."

"But I promise you that what went on with your mom and I is a very long story."

"Oh well that's good to know because I have all day."

"Listen when I first met your mom I knew that she was the love of my life but your mom was doing some extracurricular behind my back and to make matters worse she was doing it with one of my closet friends."

"And just how do you know that?"

"Because all of my home boys was talking and laughing about how she was making me look like a fool I tried to ignore them I even tried to shake that ire feeling away but I just couldn't look I was going to marry your mother until I came home from work early and caught her and my best friend in action and even then I tried to stay and forgive her but that wasn't enough she started coming home at all hours of the night telling me that she was with her girls only to find out that she was still creeping with my best friend and that was it that was the breaking point for me. But two weeks later she came running to me talking about he left her because he found out that she was pregnant with my baby now she had already made me look stupid so I most definitely wasn't going to let her steal the little dignity that I had left by taking care of another man baby. Look I know that, that was a childish move but I was young. Eight years later I hired an investigator to find you but your mom said that you or her didn't want anything to do with me but as I was leaving I spotted you and placed that necklace that you're wearing right now around your neck, gave you a kiss on the head, told you that I love you, and I left."

"I think that I remember something like that but it's been so long ago."

"Listen I know that this is a lot to lay on you but if I was for sure that you were mine you would have been well taken care of I mean when it comes to my kids I'm not a runner I'm there for all of them."

"When you say all of them how many kids are we talking about and how many women."

"Three women and four children."

"Wow and you say that my mom was the creeper!"

"Listen I'm not perfect I'm far from it but I take care of my responsibilities."

"If that was the case and you really cared to know if I were your child you had every choice to wait around until I was born and get a paternity test but you didn't so what you're not going to do is put the full blame on my mom because you could have easily had all of this figured out years ago."

"And you're right and I'm very sorry but I needed you to know that truth and I'm here now."

"Yea well I'm going to need to talk to my mom first because I think that I deserve the truth."

"Okay well you know my number you can reach me at any time."

Chapter 26

He got up and left and although I truly wanted to believe his story somethings just didn't sit right with me but I would talk to my mom about it because my next stop was her house. I grabbed my keys, hopped in my car, and pulled off. After driving for a while I pulled up in front of my mom's house and she was already sitting on the porch. I got out of the car and walked towards her and she welcomed me with open arms.

"Hey baby."

"Hey mama what you doing out here?"

"I'm just getting some fresh air I couldn't sit in the house on a beautiful day like this."

"It is quite a beautiful day."

"Yes, it is now come on over here and take a seat you ain't going to get any taller," she said gesturing at the chair sitting next to hers. I walked up the two steps and I sat in the chair.

"So did you talk to Juelz?"

"Yes we talked and we both realized that we were both wrong so everything is good now."

"That's good to know because you and Juelz are great together and I would hate to see you guys going through something so major over something so small."

"Yea I agree but mama there something I have to ask you?"

"Ok."

"I went on and took your advice and I reached out to Donald and we talked but he said some unsettling things about you."

"Like what?"

"Mama around the time that you got pregnant with me was you cheating on Donald with his best friend and should I also be looking for the other guy?"

"Listen I don't know what your daddy told you but whatever it is it can't be accurate if you're asking me a question like this. Look when I got with your dad I was head over hills for that man but after being together for a year he stopped coming home like he was supposed to and when I say that I mean sometimes I wouldn't see that man for three or four days before he showed his face to me again. Now I loved your dad and I really wanted things to work out so whatever he told me I believed it even if it was something as corny as him saying that his car broke down and he was over his friend house until it got fixed but I wanted to believe him so bad. Now over the course of two years' things had seemed to be getting better until his best friend Joe came to the house unannounced and he told me that he had been trying to stay out of our relationship but he knew that I was a good girl and that I didn't deserve what he was putting me through and that's how I found out that Donald was bringing his sluts to his office to have his way with them and when he got home he would shower and have his way with me. I was so heartbroken but he told me that if I didn't believe him that I should pop up at his job with him a lunch and then I would see. That night I contemplated on telling Donald just to see how he would react but I decided against it. Although I still hadn't done what Joe had asked of me he would come day after day with more news and more names. One day Donald got off of work early and he caught Joe leaving and he couldn't understand why Joe was there and because I didn't want him to know I lied and said that Joe was looking for him. He believed it or so I thought. I had listened to Joe long enough and I knew that he wouldn't risk his friendship with his best friend over a lie and so one day I decided to cook him lunch only to pop up at Donald's job and find a girl by the name of Paula with his cock in her mouth. I was so hurt and I didn't know what to do and he beg me to come back home and he promised that he would fix it so stupidly I went back a couple of weeks had passed and I was feeling a little weird and I went to the doctors' and found out that I was pregnant. When I left I was so excited and I was going to tell him the good news that night but then Joe came back knocking on the door and I knew that that was anything but good. I let him in and we talked and I let him know that I was pregnant only to found out that two other women was also pregnant by Donald. Oh my god I cried my eyes out and Joe was trying to console me when Donald walked in asking Joe what he was doing to me and why was I crying that's when I let him have it and I let him know everything that I knew and that I no longer wished to be with him anymore. I told him that after I gave birth he was free to see his child whenever he wanted but I wanted nothing to do with him. Only for him to tell me that it wasn't his baby and that he knew that I was sleeping around with Joe and he wanted nothing to do with me or my child. Eight years later I could say that I was a little selfish because he tried to make things right but I just didn't want him to disappoint you like he had done me now maybe that's not a good excuse but I just couldn't stomach it but I told him that me or my child didn't need him nor did we want him in our lives. Now ten years later here we are."

"So what you're telling me is that I have two siblings around the same age as me?"

"And could be more look who's to say but one thing I would never do is lie to you to make myself look good and that's exactly why when you told me about Juelz I was trying to hold you back and keep you from getting hurt because of my past experience and that was wrong of me because not every man is Donald."

"Wow it's just so much going on that I don't know what to believe."

"That's understandable but I have no problem with having a face to face with Donald so that truth can be revealed."

"That would be great how about in two days the meeting will be at the restaurant around the corner from my house."

"What time?"

"I'll call you with the information."

"So are you sure that he's going to show up?"

"Oh I know that he will."

"Ok then see you in two days."

I hopped inside my car and I drove to my girl Kiera's house. I had; had a stressful day and if anyone would take my mind off of it, it would be Kiera. When I finally pulled up to her house I noticed a strange car in her drive way. I got out of my car and I rang the doorbell now usually my friend would be ecstatic to have me over but when she opened the door instead of her opening it wide enough for me to enter she cracked it.

"Hey Royal girl."

"Hey what you doing?," I said pushing my way into the door only to find a guy sitting on the couch.

"I'm just talking to my friend Maxwell."

"Maxwell huh," I said looking at Kiera.

"Yes Maxwell this is my best friend Royal and Royal this is my friend Maxwell."

"Nice to meet you Maxwell and if you don't mind me asking how did you two meet."

"We met at work," Maxwell said.

"Yea he's one of my coworkers."

"Oh."

"Umm maybe I should go," Maxwell said.

"Yea maybe you should," I said.

"I call you later," he said to Kiera.

"Ok," Kiera said.

"If you were smart you wouldn't do that her man is one of my friends and I would hate to have to send him to your job because he's crazy so do us all a favor and forget that ya'll ever met," I said.

"Got it," he said quickly walking out the door.

"Royal?"

"Don't Royal me you're the one with a man in your house like you forgot that your man is crazy!"

"Oh really well as you can see that he's nowhere to be found and he's out there doing god knows what."

"Oh my god; did you sleep with him."

"No."

"Did you sleep with him?"

"No, but I wanted to."

"Kiera why would you even attempt to do something like that.?"

"Because I'm lonely look, Royal I'm not like you I just can't sit here trusting a secretive man not knowing what's to come"

"And just what is that supposed to mean?"

"It means that I'm not ready to put my heart on the line just so that it can be stepped allover."

"Oh so that's what you think that I'm doing"

"No Royal I didn't mean it like that I just feel that Juelz really loves you so you have nothing to worry about but Siy and I are new to this thing and you never know what he has up his sleeves, maybe he's tired of me and he want something different who's to say but I'm trying, I'm really trying but I'm just scared."

"I know that you are but as your best friend I would never do anything to put you in a bad situation and I'm telling you that he's not doing anything I promise."

"Ok I don't trust him a hundred percent but I do trust you so I'll let it go but only if you promise not to tell anybody about what happened here today."

"Girl I would never do that because Siy would kill you and I would miss my best friend."

We sat and talked and I updated her about what had been going on in my life and she was just as surprised as I was when I heard some on the things that had gone wrong in my parents' relationship. After catching up I returned home took a bath and I cooked dinner. When Juelz entered the house all of the lights was off and the only thing that you could see shining was the flame from the candles and the only aroma that he could smell was the food in the kitchen.

"Baby what's this?"

"Our makeup dinner."

"Oh I think I'm going to like this."

"Of course you will now go get ready for dinner so that mama can serve you."

He went upstairs, took off his shoes, washed his hands and he was back at the dinner table."

"So tonight we're going to be having fresh fillet salmon, spinach, with roasted red potatoes, and for dessert we will be having strawberry cheesecake."

"You definitely know how to keep your man happy."

"Yea well you know I can do a lil something; something."

"Well this pass a lil something but I'm going to enjoy it."

"Ok I'll be right back."

I went into the kitchen and I fixed both of our plates. I came back to the dining room, placed our plates on the table, said grace, and we ate and talked about both of our day. Although mine had more drama and he gave me very little detail to go off of the conversation was great. After dinner instead of me cleaning up the dishes he did them. Just as we were about to go upstairs and finish our night off the doorbell rang.

"I wonder who that could be," I said.

"I don't know but I'm going to check it you stay here."

He left for a couple of seconds and when he returned to the dining room Portia was right behind him."

"Hi Royal."

"Hey girl what's up?"

"Do you have a minute to talk?"

"Yea let's talk in the living room."

I showed her to the living room and she started spilling all the tea.

"Yesterday Trent called me. "

"Ok what's wrong with that."

"He called me from jail he'd gotten into an altercation with his wife over the girls. She was emotionally distract because they've been married for thirteen years and they've never conceived so looking at the girls whenever their around she just couldn't bare it. Anyway he ended up hitting her.

"How could a man do something like that and what was the purpose in him calling you?"

"They gave him a bond and he didn't have the money."

"Don't tell me that you bailed him out."

"I had no choice he's the father of my kids I couldn't just leave him in there."

"So what did Chase say?"

"See that's the problem I haven't gotten around to telling him yet."

"So when do you plan on telling him."

"I don't know do you think that he's going to be upset."

"I don't know; maybe I know that I would be; look I know that he's the father of your kids but you're not entitled to do anything for this man if you don't want to but I think that it's more to it than that so spill the beans."

"Ok a couple of days ago he called me and said that he was willing to leave his wife to be with me and the kids."

"What, are you crazy; what about Chase?"

"I love Chase but what if Trent and I was supposed to be together and I choose Chase over him and Chase and I don't work out."

"You can't possibly believe that you guys were met to be; I mean the whole five years that you were together he never mention that he was married and when you told him that you were pregnant he didn't even acknowledge your kids. Look I get that you want a better life and that you dream of having this family and everything but I feel deep down in my heart that Chase is the one to build that with don't lose everything that you have for a dream that has an 80% chance of crumbling in your face, I mean you seen what he did to his wife so what do you think that he will do to you. My mama always told me the way you get a man could be the same way you lose them."

"So what should I do?"

"First of all you should drop any thoughts of being with Trent, let him know that you're happy with Chase, tell him not to contact you unless it has something to do with the kids, and tell Chase the truth."

"I'm scared I don't want to lose him."

"Well you're going to have to take that chance because if he finds out from another source that's going to hurt him even more and the chance of him staying to work things out will be very small."

"I guess you're right thank you for the advice."

"What are friends for?"

"No what are sisters for?"

"Oh you're definitely my sister and there's nothing you can do about it."

"I wouldn't do anything to change it."

"Aww I love you girl and call me and let me know how everything goes."

"I love you too and I will."

She got in her car and drove off. After I was sure that the door was locked I went upstairs with Juelz.

"So what was that all about?"

"Oh nothing she just had a little situation that I helped her out with."

"And you can't tell me what that something was."

"Sister code."

"Oh I see so ya'll just threw me away huh."

"No baby we wouldn't do that but you don't have to know everything."

"That's ok because Siy and I have Bro code."

"Let me guess do ya'll talk about how bad your arm pits smell after a game of ball?" I asked laughing.

"No we talk about things."

"Like what sports?"

"I will never tell its bro code," he said laughing.

"Awww is my baby jealous?"

"Maybe a little."

"Awww do you want a kiss to make you feel better?"

"Yea I could use about a hundred of them."

"And what else?" I asked putting my hand down his pants.

"Don't get me started."

"What did I do?" I asked smiling.

"Oh you going to find out you just keep on."

The night ended well and the next morning I woke up with a smile on my face. I watched as Juelz got ready and left. An hour later the doorbell rang. I went to answer it and it was Kiera and Terri.

"Hey girl," they greeted.

"Hey ya'll come on in."

They came in and went straight into the living room but as soon as I was about to close the door Portia showed up.

"Hey girl you busy?" Portia asked.

"No but my girls just came just in case you need to speak with me in private."

"Oh no its fine can I come in."

"Yea come on in and join the party their in the living room."

She came inside and we went to join Terri and Kiera.

"Hey everyone ya'll remember my sister in law Portia."

"Yes we do how are you?" Terri and Kiera both asked.

"I'm fine and you."

"I'm fine," Terri said.

"I'm something but I just can't figure out what yet," Kiera said.

"Don't worry about Kiera she's just down because she's causing problems in her own relationship."

"Well, girl you're not alone I just might have done the same exact thing but trust me when I say it's not worth it," Portia said.

"Amen sister!" I shouted.

"Maybe not in your situation but my situation is a whole other story," Kiera replied.

"I don't know your situation but when I tell you that if you have something good you better hold on to it because once you lose that person their gone I don't care if you guys are going through problems at the time if you really love each other you stay there and work it out, I mean I wish I took heed to my own words and maybe I won't be on pins and needles with my relationship."

"So did you tell him?" I asked.

"Yea I did."

"And what did he say?"

"Well last night he didn't say anything at all and then this morning before he left he normally says I love you and I'll see you later but this morning he just said I'm off to work."

"You think he's going to leave."

"Honestly I'm not sure but if I could do anything differently I would ignore that phone call."

"Girl I don't mean to pry but what phone call?" Kiera asked.

"Really Kiera?" I asked.

"What?" Kiera asked.

"It's okay," Portia said as she began explaining everything that had went on.

"Oh wow that's a lot but I honestly feel like he's going to stay," Kiera said.

"How can you be sure?" Portia asked.

"Girl this man has accepted you and your three girls and if he really wanted to leave he could have easily called off work and packed up and left but he didn't and it's because he loves you maybe it's going to take him a while to get over it but he's not going anywhere but once ya'll get passed this be sure to keep the devil out of your relationship," Kiera said.

"I hope not and I will because this is not a good feeling," Portia said.

"Now only if you could take your own advice," I said to Kiera.

"Shut up my situation is different," Kiera said.

"The only difference is he's asking you to trust him something he's never asked before and you can't even do that because you've been in so many bad situations that you start second guessing him and the relationship and I don't think that it's fair for him to be blamed for your prior relationships," I said.

"Maybe that's true but he could give me a little insight on what he's doing because him saying it's a surprise and I will find out soon isn't going to cut it because there's a such thing as a good and bad surprise," Kiera said.

"That's true but maybe you need to sit him down and tell him that instead of trying to play behind his back and writing him off before you even know what happening," I said.

"Kiera you didn't!" Terri asked.

"No but I thought about it before Royal showed up," Kiera said.

"You keep on inviting the devil into your relationship and you going to end up losing everything that you worked for," Terri said.

"Yea, yea, yea I think I got it but I didn't come to be depressed or bored so who want to play a little truth or dare," Kiera asked.

"I'm gamed," Terri said.

"You know that I'm down," I replied.

"I guess I'll beat ya'll at your own game," Portia said

"Okay Terri truth or dare?" Kiera asked

"Dare."

"Terri I dare you to go outside, hop on one foot, and yell I wet my pants," Kiera said.

"No problem," Terri said as she went outside and did what she was told. We laughed so hard that our stomachs hurt.

"Portia truth or dare?" Terri asked.

"Dare," Portia said.

"Portia I dare you to put ice down your pants and run down and back up the street once screaming freeze pops come and get you freeze pops," Terri said.

"You're on" Portia replied and before I knew it Portia was getting ice out the freezer. But that was nothing compared to me watching her run up and down the street and trying so hard to get the ice out of her pants oh my god we laughed so hard that I almost peed myself.

"Royal truth or dare?" Portia asked.

"Dare," I responded.

"Ok because you're pregnant I'm going to have to go easy on you so Royal I dare you to call Juelz in a frantic voice and tell him that you peed your pants," Portia said.

"Okay," I said as I picked up the phone.

"Hello."

"Baby, baby!"

"Royal what's wrong?"

"I just peed my pants!"

"Really Royal."

"I'm sorry it was a dare," I said laughing.

"Oh I'm going to get you back," he said laughing.

"Baby it wasn't my fault."

"This means war."

"Okay baby I got to go I love you."

"I love you too," and with that we hung up.

"Kiera truth or dare?" I asked.

"Dare," Kiera said.

"Kiera I dare you to hold a fresh onion in your mouth for five minutes," I said.

"Really you know that I hate onions," Kiera said.

"You have to do it," I said.

Kiera went into the kitchen, chopped up some onions, and put it in her mouth and just seeing the face expression that she was making I nearly died laughing.

We continued laughing and enjoying ourselves until everyone left and once again I was alone. I was just about to go upstairs and take a nap when I realized that I had one more thing to do so I picked up the phone and I called Donald.

"Hello."

"I just wanted you to know that I spoke to my mom and she would like to have a face to face with you on Saturday."

"Okay what time?"

"I think two o'clock would be nice."

"Okay you just text me the address and I'll be there."

"Okay no problem."

And with that we ended the call. If I had to be honest it felt strange just hanging up and not saying I love you daddy. As a little girl, I always had dreamed of being a daddy's girl but I didn't know what his face looked like, I didn't know what made him happy, what made him sad, or what even made him laugh and growing up when I looked in the mirror I couldn't tell what features that I had received from him. Sitting around thinking it took me back to my tenth birthday when I sat on the porch crying after getting into an argument with my cousin as she reminded me that I didn't have a father and that I would never have a father. My eyes filled with tears for the hurt that, that little girl had endured but now that I was older and I had put a face on the man that help create me, the man I had been looking for, for most of my life I wasn't filled with joy and happiness because all I could do was ask myself why would he abandon me and what was so important that he couldn't pick up a phone and call me or even send me a card or a letter to let me know that he cared. I tried to push the thought out of my mind because I didn't want to remember that little girl because she had managed to grow to be a strong young woman without him in her life. I wiped my tears away, went in the kitchen to make me some tea, and then I went upstairs to take a nap. My nap ended up going into the night and I was awakened by a kiss on the neck

"Hi Ms. Royal how are you and my son doing/"

"Well we're a little tired and a little bit of stressed."

"Why are you stressed what's wrong?"

"This is just not the way I planned on my and Donald's relationship going I thought that we could get to know each other and get pass the past but if I find out that this whole relationship started off as a lie I'm going to be hurt and I'm not sure what I'm going to do because if he can lie about something like this what else would he lie about."

"I understand what you saying and what you're going through but our big day is coming up and I don't want you stressing when you should be happy."

"You're right and I should find another way to deal with it but it's driving me crazy, anyway what do you want to eat for dinner."

"Well, baby tonight no one will be cooking because we're ordering in and watching movies in the theater room so the question is what is it that you want to eat."

"I want Chinese."

"Well, Chinese it is."

Chapter 27

He called and ordered the food and then we grabbed a comfortable blanket, went don't stairs, and waited in the living room until the food came. Forty-five minutes later the food arrived and we went down in the theater room and found a nice movie to watch. Two days had passed and it was finally the day that I would get the truth about what had caused me to grow up fatherless. Although the meeting was in a couple of hours I still had to find something to keep me occupied so I decided to spoil myself and go to the mall. I hadn't gone in a minute and it was strange going by myself. I walked down the long halls looking through the windows of the stores to see what their items looked like before I went inside and just when I was about to go inside of one of the stores.

"Royal is that you?" he asked.

"Yea it's me Flight."

"I haven't seen you in a while and look at your baby bump."

"Yea Juelz and I are expecting."

"Yea that's nice to know, look I heard about what happened to your friends and I wanted to be there for you but I didn't know how Juelz would act."

"Yea well that's ok because he helped me stay strong."

"Is that a wedding ring that I see?"

"No it's an engagement ring but the wedding is just around the corner."

"Man I've missed out on a lot, do you think if we would have worked things out that you and I would be the ones getting married."

"No we just didn't click, look it was nice seeing you but I have to go."

"Ok I understand and congratulations."

"Thanks," I said as I walked away. You know it always tickled me to know that there was a time when you dated someone and gave them your all and he/she messed up a good thing and somehow after you manage to move on to someone better and they see it working out then they want to reminisce about the past. But my past would always be just a past because once I moved on I never looked back. I continued shopping until I was tired and afterwards I returned home. When I made it inside Juelz was just waking up.

"You have any special place that you need to be today," I asked.

"No I'm all yours."

"Good because my mom, Donald, and I are meeting up today so that I can get the truth and I'm going to need some support so I want you to come with me."

"Royal are you sure because this is more like a family issue?"

"Well soon mister you are going to be a part of the family so you might as well get used to it now the meeting is in an hour so you need to be upstairs getting ready."

"Yes mam," he said being sarcastic.

We both went upstairs, Juelz hopped in the shower to get cleaned up and I unpacked my bags and put my things where they needed to be. Forty to forty-five minutes later we were dressed and ready to go and that was good because it gave me enough time to get there before everyone else. When we finally made, it I chose an outside table and I prep myself to hear the truth. I was kind of nervous because I didn't know how the truth would affect me but I couldn't back out now. I sat there for ten minutes before Donald arrived.

"Hi baby girl," Donald said.

"Hi Donald this my fiancé Juelz and Juelz this is Donald my father."

"Nice to meet you again," Donald said.

"Like wise," Juelz responded.

"So is your mom going to show up?"

"Yea she should be here in a little while."

"Yea well I'm ready for the truth to come out."

While we were talking, I seen my mom walking towards us but she had some strange man with her.

"Hey mama," I said hugging her.

"Hey baby this is……"

"Joe," Donald said as if he was upset.

"It's a pleasure to meet you Joe," I said.

"Paris why did you bring him?" Donald asked.

"Oh what you thought that I was coming alone?" my mom asked.

"Of course I did this has nothing to do with him."

"It has everything to do with me you lying snake your daughter came here for the truth not a whole bunch of lies."

"Oh so you going to tell her how you were screwing her mother!" Donald yelled.

"I never touched Paris, Paris was a good woman and you just walked all over her like she was the scum beneath your shoe. This woman waited on you hand and foot and you couldn't keep your pants up. I had sat back and watched long enough and she needed to know the truth oh but you couldn't take it because we were friends and friends wasn't supposed to tell what you were doing behind your woman's back so you came up with a bogus lie and you told everyone that Paris and I was sleeping around and that she was pregnant with my baby not yours. You denied this child before birth!, Joe yelled back.

"Ok so I wasn't perfect but I loved Paris and instead of you keeping us together you were breaking us a part," Donald said.

"Joe had nothing to with that you did he didn't have two women calling home saying that they were pregnant at the same time as me you did, he wasn't the one selling me these pipe dreams making me believe that we would get married and grow old together while sleeping with several different women that was you, and now you come back trying to start a relationship with your daughter but everything that you're putting in her head is a lie you couldn't even stand up as a man and tell your daughter the truth. Granted you tried to be in her life eight years later and maybe I was wrong for keeping you away because instead of me hurting you I hurt her but I was only trying to protect her from all your lies and promises that I knew you wouldn't fulfill," my mom said.

"Ok I admit I wasn't a good man back then and I really wanted to get to know you but I was afraid that you would reject me so I lied," Donald said.

"What do you mean reject you, you mean the same way you rejected me?" I asked.

"Baby girl I'm sorry I should have been honest but when I spoke to Juelz and he told me that ya'll was engaged to be married I didn't want to miss out on anymore of your life, I wanted to be the man to walk you down that aisle and give you away," Donald said.

"What makes you think that you deserve to walked me down the aisle?" I asked.

"Baby girl I'm your father," Donald said.

"No you're not my father you're just a man that help make me but you've never been a father," I responded.

"I deserve that but I'm trying to turn over a new leaf and I really would like to get to know you, I want you to know your siblings, I want to know my grandson, I want to be a part of your life, I want to walk you down that aisle and give you away, and I want us to be a family," Donald said.

"Well I think that it's a little too late for that," I said.

"Baby girl please don't say that you're my first born, you going to have my first grandchild and I don't want to miss out on that," Donald pleaded.

"Royal I get that you're hurt and upset but I think you're reacting from rage and I just don't want you to do or say something that you don't mean the purpose of me doing this meeting today was for you to know the truth and you to know that I would never do anything to hurt you or cause you to grow up without a father but I think that you should go home and think things over before you make any kind of decision," my mom said.

"Maybe you're right look I'm glad that everything was straightened out but I think that it's best if I go home, rest, and think everything over," I said to everyone

"Yea I'll have her to give you guys a call," Juelz said.

We all hopped in our cars and went our own separate way. Three days later it was my wedding day. I sat in my dressing room getting my hair done by my stylist and getting my makeup down by a very great makeup artist while being surrounded by my best friends.

"Oh my god Royal I'm so happy for you are you excited?" Terri asked.

"I'm excited and nervous at the same time."

"Girl what are nervous about?" Kiera asked.

"Everyone is going to be looking at me what if I trip and fall."

"You better get up and start dancing so they will think it's all just a routine," Kiera said laughing.

"I know that's right but seriously I don't think you're going to mess up I think you're going to do great and everything is going to fall in place," Terri said.

"I hope so."

"Well we know so," Kiera said.

After I was done getting my hair and makeup done I went and got my dress and my friends helped me put it on I then put on my veil and I was ready to walk down the aisle but not before I was given the cue.

"Awww you look so beautiful," Terri and Kiera said.

"Aww thank you girls and thank you for being here."

"Girl we wouldn't have missed this day for nothing in the world," Kiera said.

"We surely wouldn't even if we weren't speaking it would have taken the devil himself to keep us away," Terri said.

"Agreed," Kiera said.

"Awww ya'll are going to make me cry."

"You better not start crying and messing up that beautiful makeup," Kiera said.

While we were talking Mrs. Marie came in and told me that it was time for me to walk down the aisle. I took a deep breath and I went out of the door. The song began to play and as I started to walk all eyes were on me and my eyes water a bit at the thought of it being me that was walking down the aisle. It seemed like it took forever but I finally made to my soon to be husband. We turned around and the pastor began to speak.

"Dearly beloved we're gather here today to join Juelz Rogers and Royal Wilkinson together as husband and wife."

I listened to the pastor give his speech and as he was doing so my palms began to get sweaty, my hands began to shake a little, and I knew that my nerves were starting to set in but all of that went away once the pastor had asked if we had written something or wished to say something before he continued.

"I wrote something for my beautiful wife," Juelz said as he unfolded his paper.

"Royal from the first time that I saw your face you took my breath away and I just knew that I had to have you. You came into my life and you changed my aspects and thoughts on everything and although we had a small bump in the road I knew that we were destined to be. Whenever I was down and I felt like I just couldn't go on you gave me hope. You push me to the limit and you made me want to do things that I never thought was possible. Baby you are the sun that peeps through the clouds and you just brighten up my life. I knew that when I met you that you were different from anyone that I had ever came across and you pushed me to greatness. Baby I know that I have a secret that you've been dying to know and I told you on this very day that it would be revealed. So, I'm here as a living testament to say that when you meet the one that God has made for you, you know it because they make you want to be a better you. when we first met, I was doing everything but living right but you changed all of that and you made me want more so when I leave the house in the morning and come back at night it's not because I'm cheating it's because my friend Siy and I are working and going to school and I can't speak for him but you made that possible for me and I just thank you for trusting in me and believing in me. Ms. Royal I love you and there's no one else that I'd rather be standing here with and passing my last name too," Juelz said.

I tried to keep it together but the tears began to roll down my face.

"Juelz when we first met I thought oh my god this man is a playa and he's trying to play me," I said laughing while the crowd also chuckled.

"But I was wrong and one night when I was stranded and didn't have nowhere else to go you my super hero came and swept me off my feet. You didn't know two things about me but you still chose to be there for me. From then on I knew that I had been avoiding the wrong man and that you were a gift from God. There was a storm that shifted my life and I wanted to give up on life but you wouldn't let me. You were my back bone, you were one of my biggest supporters, and you were my angel in disguise. You showed me that there is a such thing as true love. You made it where I didn't have to worry not just financially but emotionally. You were my strength, you were my security, and you would do anything in your power to protect me. I made it through a lot of hardship because of you. You came in and you change my life I was broken when I met you but you showed me that it was okay to love someone. I wasn't just your teacher you taught me things too and for that I came into this relationship as a young lady and I'm going into this marriage as a grown woman. Juelz, I love you and if I had to go back and do it all again there's only one thing that I would change and it would be to look at you in a different light because you are my pride and joy and you are my life," I said.

"Who gives this woman away?" The pastor asked.

"I do." Donald stood up and said.

"By the power invested in me I now pronounce Juelz Rogers and Royal Wilkinson as husband and wife you may kiss your bride."

I looked at my husband and we gave each other the most passionate kiss that we had ever given.

"Ladies and gentlemen I present to you Juelz and Royal Rogers!"

Chapter 28

We walked down the aisle together as everyone congratulated us. After we left to go to the reception. We danced, ate, some people drank, and we talked among family and friends. We partied until we couldn't party anymore and when we were done. It was off to our honeymoon in the Bahamas we went. Months later I was on my way to the hospital to give birth to my son. Hours earlier I was dancing in my living room with my girls when my water broke. Kiera rode in the ambulance with me and Terri and Portia was right behind in the car. I had called Juelz and he and Siy was on their way to the hospital from work. The pain would come and go but when it came it was unbearable I had already dilated to 6 centimeters so far so I wasn't far from giving birth. Finally, I made it to the hospital and they rushed and gave me a room so that I could dress down in the hospital gown. Not soon after had Juelz and Siy arrived. My labor was very quick because an hour later I was pushing. Thirty minutes later I welcomed Juelz the second into the world. He was 6 pounds 5 ounces and 19 inches. Just when I thought the pain was over I felt need to push again and baby girl was born. I was so surprised because out of all of these months I had been thinking that I was only pregnant with one baby. I went back and I thought about the dream that I had, had about Star holding a baby girl and for a while I didn't understand it but all this time she had been trying to tell me that I was having twins. I knew that I wanted their names to be close together but I knew that I wanted to also honor my friend so I named my baby Janae Starmeka Rogers weighing 7 pounds 7 ounces and 18 inches. Three days later I was discharged from the hospital and although I would have loved for Juelz to be the one to pick the babies and I up he had to work so Kiera was taking us home. On our way, out of the hospital we bumped into Flight.

"Hey girl I was just coming to see ya'll so that I can give you these" He said as he held out some flowers, a card, and two teddy bears one being pink and one being blue.

"Flight how did you know where I was?" I asked.

"You know the streets are talking but it was nothing like that I just wanted to show you some love," Flight said.

"Well thank you," I said.

"You welcome," he said.

"Well we have to get the babies home now but I'll see you around," I said.

"Okay" He replied

Kiera continued to push me to the car. Her and one of the nurses put the babies in their car seats and then they help put me in the passenger seat. As we pulled off I noticed that Kiera had a blank look on her face and that she was quiet.

"Kiera what's up you've been quiet since we left the hospital."

"I know that voice," Kiera said.

"What voice?" I asked.

"Flight's voice!"

"Well of course you do sweetie we used to date."

"No Royal that was the same voice that I heard that night that Star was murdered," Kiera said with tears falling down her face.